THE PIRATE QUEEN
SHUKRA DUOLOGY
BOOK 1

NINA SAXENA

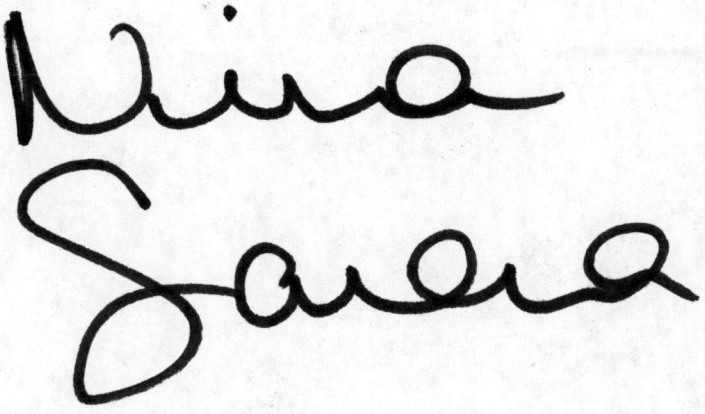

*This is my plunge into the dark. My foray into self-publishing.
Which is why it's only right to dedicate this book to the authors
who held my hand and told me it was going to be okay.
Babes, you're all rock stars.
This filthy book is for you.*

TRIGGER WARNINGS

Trigger Warnings:

- Dubious Consent (on page)
- Domestic Violence (on page)
- Rape (off page)
- Person Trafficking (off page)
- Forced Pregnancy (off page)
- Murder (on page)

PROLOGUE

Prologue: *Seven years ago*

They came for him at night when he was alone in his lab. He'd put new samples in the mass spectrometer and then gone to his mini fridge to grab his fourth soda of the shift. After returning to his seat, he spun away from the large glass windows and closed his eyes for a brief reprieve. He was the youngest scientist at the compound; a twenty-eight-year-old with a billion-dollar federal grant. According to the deep pockets funding his research, he had so much promise and opportunity to do whatever he wanted. With one phone call, he could request unlimited space, equipment, and staff.

The power wasn't important to him, though. No, it was the science.

Just as he was ready to go check on his readouts he'd been anticipating for months, lights flashed behind him, and the floor vibrated underneath his chair. The rumble became a roar that filled his ears. His heart pounded as he scrambled to his feet. Fear, an unfamiliar feeling, seized his body. If it was an earthquake, he had to get to a doorway.

He thought of his samples, of his computer with all his research. He hesitated, debating on whether or not he should save the study, or save himself. This was his life's work. This was everything he'd ever wanted, ever cared about.

A heart-stopping *boom* was the only warning before the windows blew in. He fell to the ground, glass cutting his palms and cheeks. Blinding lights forced him to hide his face in the crook of his elbow. It all happened so fast that there was no time to scramble to his feet and run for cover.

Then he felt a single prick at the base of his neck.

His body went numb, and darkness took over.

He felt a dull ache, the lingering effects from pain.

When he opened his eyes again, he instinctively knew that he'd been unconscious for a long time. As his blurry vision cleared, he heard the sounds of beeping machines, the soft hum of equipment that were unfamiliar to his trained ears. He lay under a thin sheet made of a smooth, cotton-like fabric. His head rested against the softest pillow he'd ever touched, and he wore clothes that reminded him of hospital scrubs he hadn't been wearing that morning. The room was a sterile white tomb, but the color didn't hurt his eyes.

"You're awake." The voice was a musical whisper to his left. He turned his head slightly, and the back of his neck twinged. He winced and tried to touch the spot but wasn't able to get very far since he was attached to a series of wires and tubes.

What happened?

"I'm sorry, that will be sore for a day or two. We had to

insert a serum into your brainstem to allow you to understand multiple languages."

There was a woman in a chair next to his bed. She spoke in an accent he didn't recognize. As he focused on the stranger, he registered her shiny mahogany colored hair that twisted in a complex braid. Her large eyes had a thin gold line around the iris; they were unlike anything he'd ever seen before.

He didn't know why he was so quick to come to a conclusion, but in the back of his mind he knew that she was unlike him. Unlike a *normal* person.

The machines began to beep faster. "Where am I? Who are you?" His voice was hoarse.

The woman gave him a sad smile which only succeeded in tightening his stomach in knots. Dread gripped him by the throat.

"You're on Shukra," she said softly. "About one hundred thousand light years from Earth. And I'm Queen Prita of Shukra, the monarch of the Shukra people."

He tried to sit up, but his legs were still tingling, as if his body was trying to process a poison that he'd ingested. The beeping grew louder. "This is some kind of joke, right? I'm…I'm in a facility of some kind. Have I had a psychotic break? Really, what am I doing here?" A psychotic break, he understood. He could make his way back to the life he'd built for himself if it was *just* a psychotic break.

"The rebellion retrieved you," she said. She motioned for him to stop trying to pull away from the tubes. "Deep breaths, Doctor. Let me explain."

"Please do," he said as he swallowed back the rising bile.

"We've been following your research, along with various other contraceptive studies across the known galaxies. We believe that your revolutionary antibody study can work on the Shukra people. With some adjustment, of course."

Antibodies. A contraceptive. His studies. Away from home. Shukra.

"I don't understand," he said, his voice sounding reedy and thin. "You what...*abducted* me because of my research?" He was losing his mind. He had to be. His government benefactors had isolated him after what must have been damage to his brain after the earthquake.

"Abducted is a strong word, but yes."

Abducted. There was no such thing as aliens. There was no such thing.

"I am so sorry to take you from everything you know, Doctor," the woman-like creature said softly. "But it *is* because of your research. And because somehow, on Earth, so far from my home and with such a primitive society, you are on the cusp of creating a medicine that can save me and my people."

"I'm developing a contraceptive for humans," he burst out, the machines flashing red as fear ran cold through his blood. "For all humans regardless of sex. How would our antibodies help you?"

The woman-like creature in the chair who had introduced herself as a monarch, gently tugged her cloak away from her body revealing a hugely pregnant stomach. Tears formed in her eyes even as she tilted up her chin.

"Because without a contraceptive, we'll continue to be at the mercy of those who will use us to have children. Your study, doctor, will help ensure that what is happening to me can never happen to my children."

CHAPTER 1

*P*resent day
Port City of Atlantis

Shila had complicated feelings about Atlantis. On one hand, it was a place that helped her learn what she was meant to do. On the other hand, it was too chaotic, too crowded to be considered safe for who she'd become. The merchant city bordered on lawless and attracted a certain kind of business. The only reason why Shila was back so soon after her last contract ended was because the annual boat race and sex auction at The Pleasure Chest was an opportunity for a large influx of cash. There were a lot of beings from various galaxies who would be in attendance that needed a transport business, and Shila needed the money enough to risk coming back to contract new jobs.

After scanning the private alcove she'd booked for the auction, Shila quickly sent a coded message to one of her seconds-in-command using her wrist device.

> S: You okay?

> C: Yes. Don't worry about us. Everything is under control.

She let out a breath. She had to stop thinking about her crew. They were completely capable of taking care of themselves, the ship, and anyone else who needed it.

Just as Shila was completely capable of taking care of herself, too.

She removed the small clip that held back her mass of curly black hair and pressed the discreet button on top of the hinge. The tip cast a bright red glow. Using the scanner, Shila systematically inspected the alcove. It had cost her a fortune to reserve the space, but this was the safest vantage point to observe the auction.

She knew that as an interplanetary cargo transporter who skirted intergalactic laws and politics, people were dying to use her as an informant and asset. That meant that she was stuck crawling around on her hands and knees checking for cameras, audio devices, or anything that could leak information about her location.

It was inconvenient, but her survival didn't just affect her. If Shila lived, then there was a chance that her people could, too.

Shila almost banged her head against the arm of the chaise as she shifted to her feet. "Damn," she hissed, just as the small speaker system welcomed all of the members in the private alcoves to the auction. The announcement was completed in five different galaxy languages.

Remel had explained to her once that the city was a

nexus in the cosmic universe. A pinpoint where time, realms, and planets could connect. The very fabric of life was tied in knots, and Atlantis was built upon the foundation of one of those knots. That meant there were a lot of people who could be in the same place at the same time.

Ignoring the speaker, she finished her scan. When it came up empty, she stood and brushed off her leather pants. "All clear," she murmured. Now she could do or say whatever she wanted in this room without worrying about someone shoving a knife into her back.

She clipped her hair with the discreet sensor again and sunk into the deep plush red leather couch positioned in front of the one-way mirror. Since her safety checks were done, she could finally relax.

Most beings would love to be in her boots. Getting tickets to the annual auction meant she had a front-row seat to debauchery for the highest price.

When the auction started, she'd have a drink and watch the betters to see who would leave with their money pouches intact. The predictable fools with their fast toys and currency to burn. After the races, they always came to The Pleasure Chest looking to leave the port city with a bang. Literally. And those who lost the auction were ripe for the picking in Shila's opinion.

At last year's auction, she'd made one hundred and fifteen million rupa. It was enough for her and her crew to buy supplies for Shukra people in the rebellion, while also shoring up her savings. This time, she was hoping for more.

She wanted enough for her own port town where she felt safe. Where her crew, and other exiled Shukra, felt safe. She'd found another nexus point hidden in a corner of the Rahu region, and it could be hers.

Just a few hundred million more rupa to go.

There was a knock on her alcove door, and the server assigned to Shila appeared a moment later and locked the entrance behind them. They didn't say a word as Shila returned her knife to its holster at her ankle.

The being was stunning, with a narrow, teardrop face and a shiny silver bald head. Their ribbon-like tail whipped back and forth in a lazy arc. They had the markers of originating from the Bhu Galaxy.

"My lady." The being approached Shila with a large saucer filled with bottles that held various neon-hued liquids. The tight leather of their bodysuit shifted with a soft hush as they presented the saucer. "Remel has poured your drink themselves for your safety. They also wanted to give you a message." The server handed her a piece of parchment sealed with melted wax.

"Thank you," Shila said. She motioned to the small black onyx table next to the couch. "Leave it there." Then, with one quick flick of the same knife she'd used moments before, she cut the seal to read the bold letters scrawled across the parchment.

You're a pain in my ass.

Shila grinned. "Love you, too, Remel," she mused. She was pretty sure she wouldn't have time to see them on this visit, but she'd have to stop by their fortress soon. As Atlantis's ruler, owner, whatever title they liked to be called on any given day, Remel had enough power to ensure that no one would question their actions in protecting her.

She'd never had an older sibling, but she imagined that if she did, they would be like Remel.

"My lady?" the being said, their hands folded in front of them. Their eyes were in the shape of round orbs as they stared down at her. "I am here to service you as well. In any way you'd like."

Shila practically rolled her eyes. She waved the server away to the side so she could watch the auction. The lights had dimmed, and creatures in the viewing seats were chanting for the show to begin.

It wasn't the first time she'd received an offer like this. She was an exiled princess who'd taken a vow to never mate with a seeder. Even though her oath was limited to those who had the capacity to impregnate her, once word got out, the attempts to seduce her had gotten bolder with each individual who wanted her. She was easy to recognize with her height, her breasts, and the gold ring around her iris. That was why she preferred isolation.

She'd never been tempted to break her oath and preferred to seek pleasure with beings who were other breeders or who she'd never have a child with. There was too much at stake for her to introduce a child into this world. A child she'd love but never want.

"I have taken a vow—"

"—of celibacy from mating with seeders, yes I know," the being said. "But I am not a seeder. Remel wanted to send a gift to you. I volunteered to be your gift. I assure you that anatomically, we are quite compatible."

"Remel wouldn't—"

At that same moment, her time device blinked with an incoming coded message.

> R: You need to loosen up. Ray-ten has the highest security clearance. An alternate dimension being. They are omni.

"Well then," Shila murmured. Her doubt transformed into curiosity. Even though the majority of humanoids were breeders or seeders, there were thousands of sexes in alternate galaxies and dimensions. An omni was one of them. Shila would be safe from complications if they were to share pleasure. Omni's reproduced on their own.

More importantly, she could trust the information if it came from Remel.

She picked up one of the bottles on the tray and twisted off the topper before tossing it aside. With one long look at the server, she swirled the blue-hued liquid and took a long sip. There was a warm burning sensation that heated her blood.

It *had* been a long time. Her last mission was a harrowing experience, and she'd been running on adrenaline for so long. Maybe if she had a chance to release some…energy, she'd be able to focus on digging into those deep pockets she'd come for. And this being was beautiful. If they worked for Remel, they usually were.

"If you still have doubts, you may inspect me if you'd like." The being reached to their side and made quick work of undoing the zipper that held together the leather bodysuit. Within seconds they were naked. Although they appeared relatively humanoid, with breasts and familiar extremities, there were subtle differences—from the eyes to the tail. Their skin glinted in the dim lighting, a shimmery silver and titanium color. A nub protruded through their thick folds at the top of their mound. From her place on the couch, Shila could see that it vibrated in a rotating motion.

A personal, live device native to the Bhu quadrant. Perfect.

Shila could feel her own pleasure center grow hot and wet with interest. Damn, Remel. She'd owe them for this.

Behind the being, through the mirror, an old woman with stark-white hair stood in the middle of a dark grey stage surrounded by sparkling light fixtures. She moved into the brightest spotlight and spun in a slow circle.

Eloise, the proprietor of the brothel next door, lifted a microphone to her mouth as the crowd at the base of the stage, the spectators who didn't have two rupa to rub together, began to quiet. "Welcome to The Pleasure Chest's annual sex auction, you horny bastards!"

Shila listened to Eloise's speech, registering the new rules, even as she removed the sensor clip from her hair and shook her curls loose for a second time. The being standing in her view shifted, the nub beckoning her to ride it.

She crooked two fingers at the being, motioning them closer. "Your name is Ray-ten?"

"Yes."

"Ray-ten." The name rolled off Shila's tongue again as she savored it. She reached out and touched the nub with her thumb. It was firm, resisting the stroke of her finger.

What the hell? Why not?

She pinched the nub hard, and Ray-ten jerked with a gasp.

"Remove my clothes," Shila said, her voice as sharp as one of her throwing knives. "Do so quickly so I can fuck you and focus on more important matters. And if you so much as think of using my weapons against me, your blood will spill over this carpet. Understood?"

"Yes, milady," Ray-ten said. They were breathing heavily, their mouth wet, their eyes round and bulbus.

It took a few seconds for Ray-ten to pull Shila to her feet and begin removing all her layers. Then came the knives, the laser shooters, and the interior layers of leather that formed a pile at the end of the couch.

At six one, Shila towered over the being with her high and firm breasts, wide hips, and a toned, muscled body stronger than most warriors. Ray-ten seemed to appreciate her form as they used their tail to stroke over her bare skin. The touch was strange but left a streak of sensation in its wake, which only proceeded to make Shila wetter.

Over Ray-ten's head, she watched as the first auction participant stepped onto the stage. A minotaur. Their horns were wide and as broad as their shoulders. Their abdomen was a ripple of muscle, coded with a thick mat of body hair.

"We shall start the bidding at ten thousand rupa," Eloise called out. The intergalactic currency meant the minotaur was open to going off planet and away from their realm.

Red lights turned on over a few one-way mirrors circling the stage. Shila gasped as Ray-ten got to their knees, pushed Shila's legs apart and after separating her folds with gentle fingertips, began licking her pussy with precise, practiced strokes.

That was when she discovered the other being's tongue was as long and flexible as their tail.

She hooked a leg over Ray-ten's shoulder, balancing on her bare feet. Her boots lay discarded next to them.

"Yes, what a good lover you are," Shila whispered,

stroking the bald head that was between her thighs. She groaned in pleasure as their tongue reached deep inside her and Ray-ten's tail came around to stroke Shila's anus.

Her legs trembled as she rode Ray-ten's mouth, feeling the soft pressure against her asshole as the tail stroked her to the same rhythm as the long, sinuous tongue. Gods, she loved when her pussy got the attention it deserved. The feel of sharp pleasure, the rising ache deep in her core, and the way she grew wetter with each attentive stroke.

Shila dropped one foot to the floor, then clasped her hands on both sides of Ray-ten's head and brought them up to their feet so they stood face to face. She leaned down to kiss Ray-ten for the first time, to feel that talented tongue in her mouth. Their breasts brushed, and hard nipples teased each other as they pressed close. Hands raced down bare muscled backs, over smooth, curved butt cheeks. Ray-ten's tail continued to tease Shila's pussy from behind, and she gasped into the being's mouth.

"Get on the couch," she growled. She'd waited long enough. Ray-ten went to comply, rubbing her nakedness against Shila one last time before she sat on the cool leather, and lay down. In invitation, she pressed one heeled foot to the floor while the other hooked over the back of the couch.

"Sold to alcove twenty-two for fifty thousand rupa!" Eloise called out. "Participants will be led to the holding room where they will wait until payments are received. Then Golda, the owner of this fine establishment, will handle payments. Let's bring out participant number two!"

The sounds of bidding faded as Shila lowered herself onto Ray-ten's prone form, positioning her pleasure center over the protruding nub that was already gyrating in a circular motion. When that muscle parted her slit and began moving over her clitoris, Shila let out a groan just as Ray-ten gasped in pleasure.

"Do you like this, Ray-ten?" Shila said, rolling her hips in time to the moving nub. She nipped at that sharp, pointed chin, then to sooth the pain, she licked the spot with her tongue.

"Y-yes, my lady." There was a note of hesitancy in their voice. "But you c-can go harder?"

Shila groaned at the words, then leaned back so she could slap one of Ray-ten's breasts to watch it bounce. "You like a little pain, do you?" Shila whispered as she rubbed against the deliciously firm, vibrating nub at a faster speed.

Ray-ten's gripped Shila's hips. "Y-yes, my lady."

"Sold!" Eloise called out, sounding hollower in the distance as Shila began fucking the being in earnest now. When she gripped Ray-ten's throat and squeezed, Ray-ten's eyes bulged; they hissed, gasped, and then thrust up from under Shila, a keening sound coming from their mouth.

They bucked against each other on the couch, their shouts growing in volume. Release was just on the horizon. Shila could feel it rising inside her. It had been long, so very long since she'd had a release of her own.

Almost there. Hurry, hurry, hurry.

She closed her eyes, fucking Ray-ten until a thin sheen of sweat formed over their bodies, their cries melding, as Shila held Ray-ten's neck firmly in her hand.

"Participant five will accept rupa or one...ah, yatra?"

Yatra.

As if someone had doused her with ice water, she froze, even as Ray-ten screamed in protest under her. Shila put pressure on their neck. "Hold," she snapped. Then she stumbled off the couch naked to approach the window. She hadn't heard that word in almost ten years. Eloise must've been mistaken.

"One yatra!" Eloise called out again.

No. No way.

The participant who had claimed to want a yatra stood shirtless next to Eloise in thin-fabric pants and bare feet. They were human. That was clear in the rugged features of their face, the early growth of a thick beard, and their wavy hair. Their skin was a dark brown but dull in color, as if they hadn't spent enough hours in proximity to a UV ray source. It stretched over taut muscled arms, back and squared shoulders.

When the human turned in a circle, glancing at the audience on the floor and up at the alcoves, Shila saw the barest hint of injection marks at the base of his neck.

Lights turned on above the other alcoves, the inhabitants shielded behind mirror glass.

Shila didn't think twice. She immediately pressed the button next to the window, turning her own red light on.

"Okay, we have a few bidders!" Eloise called out. "Ten thousand rupa and…two yatra?"

When the participant shook his head and lifted a finger to signal one yatra instead, Shila knew he was very aware of what a yatra meant. She slammed the button again.

"Fifteen thousand rupa and one yatra!"

"Twenty thousand rupa and one yatra!"

When none of the other lights flickered on, Shila's heartbeat slowed.

"Going once, going twice, sold to alcove nine!"

The human looked up, their dark grey and brown eyes looking at the mirrored glass. Their steady stare made it appear as if they could see Shila and her naked form.

"My lady, you won."

Ray-ten's voice cut through Shila's trance. She turned to see the naked body, the throbbing nub, and the slick sheen across those pert silver breasts. The tail was now teasing the nub as Ray-ten pleasured themself.

Shila knew it would have to wait to collect her winnings. It would be too risky to arrive and chance running into any number of enemies. And then there was her need to find the losing bidders.

With newly developed tension in her muscles, she needed release as much as Ray-ten wanted it. She crossed the alcove naked, her hair a halo around her head. "I will take your body until I am done with you. Then you will clean me with your mouth and dress me before I leave."

The high-pitched keening sound came from Ray-ten's throat again. "Yes, m-mistress."

Shila climbed on the being again and centered her pleasure center over the nub. Soon they were thrusting hard against each other, with Shila lifting Ray-ten's hips to fit against her. They fucked until the walls shook with their screams. Then Shila was cleaned up with Ray-ten's mouth as instructed, carefully dressed, and escorted to the holding rooms.

Although she'd participated in a sex auction, there was no way Shila would be taking pleasure from her winnings, too. She'd had a few rare encounters with humans, and there was a very good chance upon initial inspection that this being was a seeder. She'd taken an oath, and a Queen, exiled or not, never turned back on her word.

CHAPTER 2

It had been exactly forty-eight hours since Vahman's getaway cruiser crashed near a forested area on Atlantis. He'd been detained by a fae security guard, processed in a room as sterile and icy as a morgue, and had a conversation with the first human he'd seen in seven years.

Or was the person half human?

Whatever he was, the being claimed to be a priest who wanted to understand what Vahman was doing on Atlantis and why he was carrying ten vials in a leather medical bag.

When he'd discovered that Vahman was looking for the Pirate Queen, he combed his fingers through his shoulder-length sandy blond hair, straightened his Hawaiian shirt, and put a stop to the interrogation. All the guards left, and the doors opened. Then the priest offered him a private room above the church to stay and a few days of provisions until he found what he was looking for.

Unfortunately, that was the last help Vahman had received from a local.

"Name and participant number?" the humanoid woman with the soft jaw and black hair asked. She stood behind a large desk, an old-fashioned clipboard in hand. Her clothes were almost medieval in style, a combination of buckskin and leather, but her glare was all too fresh.

"Vahman Raj," he said. "Human from the Rahu region. Participant number five. I believe my winner was in alcove nine."

The woman looked up from her paper, eyebrows twitching at the mention of the alcove number. "No, I don't think…" After checking the tablet once more, then twice, her mouth closed, lips thinning. "I'll be damned. I guess it was alcove nine. What is she up to?"

A feeling of dread, a sensation that had kept him up every night since his abduction, churned in his gut. "The Pirate Queen? Is that who it was?"

The woman dropped her clipboard to the table. The loud clatter echoed through the room. "You'll find out soon enough."

Vahman wanted to snap back. That seemed to be everyone's response when he asked for the Pirate Queen. No one was willing to speak to him, or to share how he could find her. Not the shopkeepers, the people in the square, the people in the local tavern, or even the priest himself. Vahman was wasting valuable time all because this exiled royal, Prita's estranged sister, was protected. What had she done to earn their trust? Or was it their fear?

Vahman knew next to nothing about her. Prita rarely spoke of anything but their research. However, just before she'd locked him in the cruiser and input the coordinates for this port city, she'd told him to trust her with the truth. With who he was, and what he needed.

"You'll wait over there to the side until your winner, or

whatever crew member she sends to pick you up, can retrieve you," the woman said, pointing to a corner. "Damn, I'm going to lose money on this. I can feel it. Let me get your clothes."

Vahman waited for her to retrieve his canvas bag from behind a hidden panel.

Gripping the soft fabric in his fingers eased some of the frustration and adrenaline that coursed through his veins. His desperation to find the Pirate Queen led him to the sex auction as his last resort. He'd seen the flyer that morning as he walked through town looking for help. If this didn't work…well, he'd be the sex servant of God knows what monster for three days.

Three days where he was forced to act in whatever depraved way his winner demanded. That was the timeline he'd committed to when he enlisted.

The only upside was that if he survived his contractual obligation, then at least he'd have money. He'd receive 70 percent of the profits, and 70 percent of twenty thousand rupa might be enough to keep him safe until he could find another exit strategy.

"Here," the woman said when she came back with his bag. "Now go on."

He nodded, then fisted the straps in his hand and walked a few steps away before he looked inside to make sure all of his belongings were intact. He'd kept the chip with his years of research hidden under the thin leather strap he wore around one wrist. Everything else was disposable. But that didn't mean he was willing to let go of his things easily.

His boots, tunic, socks, and the ten vials were all there.

He sat on the plush couch and put back on his tunic and boots that he'd been told to remove prior to ascending the stage. When he was fully dressed again, he settled in to wait.

One by one, more beings entered the holding room until the space was crowded with both winners and participants. Music thrummed, a heavy erotic beat. The lights dimmed, and the walls pulsed with a red glow. Waitstaff in various forms began to pass out drinks as some winners and participants retreated to corners right inside the lounge.

Vahman stood against the back wall, watching the exchange of money and the sometimes-rough handling of participants before they dispersed into shadowed corners of the red-toned room.

After another hour passed, Vahman was sure he'd been forgotten. He was the only participant who had not been retrieved by their winner. Sounds of pleasure mixed with the music as he sat alone and watched debauchery began to unfold around him. Participants from the auction were starting to lose their clothes and crawled into the laps of their winners. Wine flowed freely, and their sighs were audible.

He shouldn't be distracted, couldn't afford it, but it had been so long for him.

That's when a being wearing a black leather bodysuit strode into the room. They were bald with silvery skin and had a tail that stretched to their ankles.

Even though he'd been abducted and then lived on an alien planet for seven years, he'd spent the entirety of that time in an underground lab. This was all so new to him that he had to work hard to control his expression.

The being went straight to The Pleasure Chest's owner manning the table. After a brief conversation, the woman pointed in his direction.

The being approached him, bulbus eyes void of emotion. They stopped in front of Vahman, hands folded. "Are you participant five?"

"I am," he said, straightening and adjusting his bag on his shoulder. His stomach knotted. "But you aren't the Pirate Queen."

The being cocked their head. "That is correct."

"Who are you then?"

"Ray-ten." Then they added, "I will deliver you to the Pirate Queen. Mistress would first like to know where you are staying. She will meet you there."

It worked, Vahman thought. His one act of desperation to find the Pirate Queen actually worked. He let out a deep shuddering breath, unbothered that whoever this person was could witness his relief. "I'm staying above the church."

The being didn't so much as blink at his retort. Instead, they lifted a square device that looked like a thin, square cell phone and typed in a quick message. The device beeped a moment later, and Vahman knew that it had to be a response.

"Follow me," the being said as they somehow managed to tuck the device into a side pocket of their skintight jumpsuit. "I will take you to the mistress."

Finally.

They had reached the doors when the owner called out, "Ray-ten, you better tell her that she owes me money, otherwise I'm coming for you both, ya hear?"

Ray-ten didn't even pause in her stride out the door, so Vahman followed suit.

They walked through the dark, narrow hallway through a labyrinth of rooms, and under two archways before they pushed through a set of heavy double doors made up of a material similar to wood back home. Vahman's heart ached when he touched it, and he was tempted to stay just to feel its grainy texture under his hand for a bit longer. He hadn't had the time to appreciate the small things when he'd first landed, and if the Pirate Queen was as ruthless as her reputation, he didn't know how much longer he'd be alive to appreciate them again.

Ray-ten led him into the bustling night of Atlantis. She walked around buildings behind the theatre towards the giant square with vehicles, carts, and crowds. The first night Vahman saw the square like this, he'd been stunned. It was all so chaotic, so...*normal*.

He stayed close to Ray-ten as they circled a couple and walked towards the church. Or what looked like a church. Vahman recognized the steeple at the entrance and the large domes on either side in gold metal as religious architecture from different countries on Earth. Back home, they wouldn't have made sense together, but here, it worked. In the center of the archway was a set of wide double doors under a glass mosaic.

"I'm staying in the room to the left—"

"She knows," Ray-ten replied.

"Of course, she does," he murmured. Vahman entered the cavernous space filled with rows of pews behind Ray-ten. There were no statues, no markers of a higher being in any art. In the eerie quiet, the stained glass in the roof created a circular design along the center aisle. In the front of the room, a large stone altar sat under a beam of moonlight on an elevated stage.

Ray-ten made a left and walked along the back of the room until she approached the dark corner.

"Oh, I can put in the code that I was given—"

Ray-ten flipped up a panel cover, then, using biometrics, unlocked a door. It quietly slid open. They turned around to look at Vahman. "I have the code."

The fact that more than one person knew how to get into the room he'd been staying in should've frightened him, but he was so tired, exhausted, to have come this far. It didn't even matter to him at this point.

"Mistress has instructed me to direct you to the second level alone, while I return to our monarch."

"Oh. Ah, okay."

Vahman peered inside the dark opening. He'd left the lights on before he'd gone to The Pleasure Chest, but now there was only darkness at the top of the staircase. Great. He hoped Prita wasn't wrong about her sister's feelings about their people. Otherwise, their plan was dead in the water before it even began.

He stepped forward, and the stair let out a loud creak that fractured the silence.

"Wonderful," he whispered.

When he had made it three steps, the panel slid closed, and he was engulfed in darkness.

"Fear," a husky, whisky-laced voice said, "is a good thing." The sound was like a hot streak of lightning straight through his skin.

I have no choice but to keep moving forward. He took a few more steps, using his hands to guide the way along the walls.

"Do you speak?"

Vahman rolled his eyes. "I do," he finally said. "You are the Pirate Queen."

"I've never heard of her," the voice said smoothly.

Chills ran over the nape of his neck. He wondered what this voice would sound like saying his name.

He took a few more tentative steps until he felt a soft

breeze. He had to be close to the top. "Prita said you were a little dramatic."

There was a long pause, and for a moment, Vahman thought maybe he'd imagined the voice and he was alone after all. His eyes began adjusting to the shadows, and he had barely enough time to register the form that stepped in front of him before an arm looped around his neck, thick, muscled, and powerful. It dragged him across the floor and shoved him into a cold metal chair. His canvas tote dropped with a thud to the floor.

A single bulb flicked on and swayed over his head. Vahman's eyes burned as he tried to take a few wheezing breaths of air. He could still feel the pressure against his throat.

When his vision adjusted, he was faced with the most gorgeous being he'd ever seen. In the swinging light, the Pirate Queen was the fallen goddess her planet claimed her to be. Her thick black hair clouded around her shoulders, mussed as if she'd been freshly fucked. Her white tunic was unbuttoned to the center of thick round breasts. Her leather pants were fitted against muscled thighs and legs that stretched for miles. She was his height in those boots, barely two inches shorter than when she was barefoot.

Like other Shukra people, she was tall and thick, her skin a deep golden brown. What set this one apart was her eyes, so big and mosaic with a ring of gold around the black, they could drown a man's soul.

His assessment was cut short when she reached forward and gripped his hair at the back of his head, then tugged until he was looking up.

"Who are you?" she snapped, those irises glowing in

anger. "And how dare you come here, asking for a yatra? Do you even know what the means?"

"Let me go," Vahman said in as calm of a tone as he could. "And I'll tell you a story about how I spent the past seven years in a Shukra lab away from the king's watchful eyes."

Because he was now able to see, he could register the shock on the woman's face.

"What did you say?" she whispered.

"Have a seat, Pirate Queen. Let me catch you up on what's been happening in Shukra. That is if you care at all."

She looked wary at first but then stood at her full height. She scanned the sparsely decorated room, from the bed in the corner under the window, to the small couch and flat screen monitor against the wall. Then she spotted another chair in the corner and crossed the room to retrieve it. She dragged it behind her, then flipped it around.

She straddled it, leaning along the backrest with her arms folded on top of each other. "Speak, human. But first, where did you hear the word *yatra*?"

Vahman nodded and placed his hands on his thighs. They carried scars now, and each one triggered a memory of the first few months when he'd refused to cooperate. "Prita told me. She explained that it was an official request for help. I could only ask for one yatra from a member of the Shukra royal family and they are bound to fulfill my request. I had no choice but to use it as a form of currency in the sex auction when none of the locals would share how to get in touch with you."

Her lips thinned. "Very economical of you. How did

you meet…" She cleared her throat. "How did you meet my sister, Prita?"

He wanted to say that if she still considered Prita a sister, maybe it would've been nice to return to Shukra and fight for her. But he needed this exiled woman's help right now, and his bitterness had no place in their negotiations.

Instead, he rubbed his damp palms against his slacks. He hadn't told his life story in a while. Another man might have even forgotten where he'd come from. Might have forgotten the names and faces of loved ones they hadn't seen for seven years. Vahman remembered everything. His brain could recall the smallest detail about his parents' appearance, about the things they said, the moments from his childhood that made him feel loved. He hadn't lived with them since he was a young teenager, so the memories were sparse after a certain age, but no less meaningful. He cleared his throat. "I was born in the United States, a country on Earth."

"The cursed planet, Rahu region," the Pirate Queen said. She nodded slowly, as if she understood more than what he was telling her. Her wild curling hair was clipped back with what looked like a discrete sensor device, and as she rested an ankle on her knee, he saw the glint of steel. "I know it's location well," she continued. "There is a port town next to your galaxy."

"Yes," he said. "Earth is class four, generally ignorant of life in space, except for a select few. As a child, I showed signs of being gifted, and after extensive testing, my family was told I possessed immense intelligence that could contribute to the development of either scientific or artistic fields."

The Pirate Queen's stoic expression was so steady that it was as if her beauty was carved in marble.

"I chose science, and with the support of our government, and other financial benefactors, I graduated from our human education system with the highest degree we can possess, at the top of my class. I was twenty-three." The memories of his youth, of his time with his friends, and his classmates through his PhD program, were just as sharp as his memories of family. He had plans to make more memories with them. To find a partner, to start a family, and to have adventures. Vahman swallowed the bitterness of knowing his life had been stolen from him. His opportunity for a future was destroyed. The only sanity he had since he'd been abducted was his science. The work he completed.

His hands fisted on his thighs.

"What does your childhood have to do with your time on Shukra?" the Pirate Queen asked, interrupting his thoughts.

"In my last few years of my education, I became interested in reproductive technology."

There was a tick at the corner of her mouth now.

"It started with an interest in antibodies, then grew into solving problems pertaining to contraception. I had no real social or moral reason for pursuing my field, other than an innate curiosity. Five years after I began my research, I was finally able to secure a grant at a federal-run lab with unlimited resources. My goal was to create a single-dose oral contraceptive using human antibodies that was effective on individuals from any sex."

"Any sex?"

"Yes," Vahman said, then realized he had to translate the word into something that she would understand. "Beings that are seeders, breeders, omni or any other humanoid reproductive designation. Anyone can take the contraceptive dose, and it will stop attempts at fertilization."

Lines formed between her brows. The Pirate Queen sat straight up, her arms falling to her side. "My people have already searched the galaxies for a cure. The human preventative methods are the least effective. Your condoms, injections, inserted devices, or surgeries don't work on us. Three days after mating, there is always a pregnancy."

"My research was revolutionary," Vahman said, without artifice. "I was already seeing promising results when I was abducted one night in my lab. I was taken to Shukra and hidden in an underground facility that had been built in secret by your sister, Prita. Her goal was to ensure that the contraceptive could save the Shukra people, too. The antibodies—human antibodies—were the first of its kind that was affecting Shukra reproductive organs. She said her people were ravaged by seeders, trafficked to other planets, and used to produce offspring against their will."

"I know what was done to my people, human," the Pirate Queen snapped. For the first time since they sat across from each other, Vahman saw a blaze of anger ignite in her irises.

"But you don't know that my work was going to be Prita's salvation."

The Pirate Queen vaulted to her feet, kicking the chair away from her. It crashed loud and hard against the wall, the wood splintering.

"Prita was the smartest of our scientists. She would know that her attempt at protecting our people is a waste. If she wanted a cure, then she shouldn't have chosen to marry that Brihaspathi scum."

"He hurts her," Vahman snapped. Images of the woman emaciated and fatigued, with dark bruises under her eyes, a protective hand, curved after so many breaks, hovering over her protruding belly flashed in his mind.

The Pirate Queen froze. Her eyes became glassy. "W-what did you say?"

"Your sister was my captor," Vahman started evenly, even though rage was coursing through his body as he thought of Prita. "I *hated* her for it. But I saw what that monster did to her. Using her as a punching bag until she was constantly in casts or slings, or with some sort of mobility device because of the broken bones and bruises. I refused to cooperate for weeks after my arrival on the planet, until I saw what she was going through and I knew she was just trying to survive, too. If Prita didn't do something, she was going to die."

The woman in front of him crossed her arms over her chest. She looked pale now, her eyes glassy with unshed tears. "Why are you here now? How did you get to Atlantis?"

Vahman slowly got to his feet until he was eye level with the Pirate Queen. He reached out, his knuckles brushing the back of her hand. "Your sister managed to keep her lab a secret for seven years," Vahman said. "Mostly because her husband would return to his planet frequently, leaving her to rule the Shukra people as she chose. But two nights ago, everything changed. I was finalizing our last round of studies, when she came running in to meet me. She'd gotten word from one of the members of the rebellion that there was a leak in the lab, and Brihaspathi soldiers were coming to destroy all of it."

The Pirate Queen's eyes widened, her mouth gaping. "Prita. Is she—"

"I'm sorry," Vahman said. He shook his head. "I don't know. I grabbed what I could from my station before she shoved me into an escape cruiser and pre-programmed the coordinates. I was told to take a serum once I was in the atmosphere that would keep me alive during the transfer to the different dimension. Right before my ship door closed, she told me I needed to find you so you could help me finish my research. Then, in exchange, you would take me home." The boon. The yatra was his key.

Vahman picked up his canvas tote. He pulled out the vials and flipped open the lid to the protective bag that held them in place.

The Pirate Queen looked down at his vials, then shook her head. "I transport goods. Sometimes illegally. I don't have access to a lab to help you finish your research like Prita wanted."

"I don't need your help. All you have to do is fulfill the yatra and get me home."

The woman looked up from the vial he held out. "That's not how this works, human—"

"You don't have to help," he continued. "Because I actually completed my research."

She cocked her head, and the gold ring around her iris glinted. "What does that mean?"

He picked up her hand and placed a vial in the center of her palm and closed her fingers around it. "I mean," he started, his heart pounding in a rapid staccato, "I created a contraceptive that works on all humanoid beings. The Shukra people, and any being from the nine galaxies created with similar reproductive organs, can have freedom from the sexual violence that results in forced pregnancy. They can reclaim bodily autonomy. Pirate

Queen, I've completed my research and have officially fulfilled my end of the bargain."

CHAPTER 3

"Do you think he's telling the truth?" Cecil asked. They held the small orb-like vial with the tablespoon of clear liquid inside between their forefinger and thumb.

"His story is definitely the strangest one I've heard," Fanna said. She reached out and took the vial from Cecil to inspect it for herself.

Shila and her seconds-in-command stood in the Captain's Dome at the heart of their ship. Shaped like a yolk with one-hundred-and-eighty-degree periphery, there were four chairs and a raised comms table in the center for outgoing calls. The ship's camouflage shield covered their location near the Atlantis woods at the rear of the docking station for intergalactic transport ships. Because she was home, Shila was able to relax and think despite the chaotic turn of events for the day.

"If what this human is saying is true," Shila started, "the contraceptive can be worth a lot of money. We can use it as a form of commerce so that Shukra people wouldn't have to rely on other invading planets for protection and financial support." It would also be the perfect bartering tool to save her sister. She never thought she'd go back after her exile, but if what the human said was right, then her knives would be coated in Brihaspathi blood soon enough.

"We should start making calls," Fanna said. She pushed her long reddish-brown braid over one shoulder and marched over to the comms panel to pull up a series of symbols and numbers on a projector in the center of the dome. A list of all the members of the rebellion and their locations populated on the screen. Someone would know how to help.

"Wait, don't you want to know if it works first?" Cecil asked. "We'd all have a death sentence if we promise a contraceptive for breeders, and it ends up being a hoax. And I'm not talking about 'you owe us money' death sentences—the Intergalactic Congress will get involved, and we'll be as good as star dust."

Shila looked up from the vial, rolling the pretty glass in her hand. So many secrets in something so unassuming. She hadn't been able to talk to her sister since her exile, but they'd still managed to communicate. Shila had been funding the rebellion since she received her first transport payout. How had she not known about Prita's research?

"How do you propose we test it?" Shila finally said. "We don't have access to a lab. And if we're talking about using it, that's out of the question, too. There's no artificial insemination facility, and most of the humanoid breeders on Atlantis have different gestation periods. That's if it's the right time for their cycle."

Cecil and Fanna looked at each other, then back at Shila. There was something in their expression that Shila was pretty sure she wasn't going to like.

"What is it?"

"One of us can try it," Fanna said slowly.

"That's out of the question." Shila shoved the vial in the satchel at her hip.

"Don't be dramatic, Shila," Cecil said. They crossed their arms over their chest plate, bracing their booted feet as if squaring off. "The solution is simple. One of us takes the contraceptive, we mate with a seeder, then wait three days."

Because Shukra people could get pregnant at any time, regardless of cycle, and pregnancy could be confirmed in three days, it was easy to test a contraceptive on themselves. But it was so dangerous, too.

"And what if it doesn't work?" Shila asked. She stepped closer to Cecil until their noses were practically touching. "Do you want to be stuck with a hybrid *child* on board a ship where we're constantly looking over our shoulders? We're all here because we want to choose when and how and if offspring are the right choice for our future!"

Fanna put a hand on both Shila's and Cecil's shoulders. Her expression was soft, and pleading. "Shila, this could be life changing for us. For the people we've left behind and for the rest of the breeder people who have suffered oppressive laws and violations of their freedom. We've faced death before for much less. I joined the rebellion because of what happened to my mother, brother, and sister. Cecil was exiled because they also killed the monster trying to take them. We've experienced so much worse than a failed contraceptive. I think one of us should try it. The question is which seeder would be safe enough to mate with?"

Shila immediately thought of the human. He was beautiful in a scarred and stern way she always found attractive. He was the perfect match to test the contraceptive. He'd also given his services away at a sex auction, so he knew what the ramifications could be.

But the idea of him mating with the crew planted two complicated feelings in her gut. One of desire to see the way he would mate with another. Serious, and with complete concentration. And the other feeling was a tinge of jealousy, as she had taken a vow and couldn't volunteer herself. Not without breaking a blood bond.

"The human asked for a yatra in exchange for safe passage back home," Shila mused.

Cecil's eyebrows jerked. "A royal call for help. He really is telling the truth."

"I think so," Shila said. "And because he has just as much at stake as we do, he'll be our seeder." She would not let emotion affect sound judgment here. There was too much on the line.

Including her sister.

It was now time to take a more active role in the rebellion. Especially if her sister's husband discovered her plans, It would be impossible for Prita to do anything without his approval now.

"I volunteer," Fanna said. There was a tick at the corner of her mouth.

Cecil snorted. "That was quick."

Fanna shrugged. "I have always wondered what it would be like to mate with a breeder, even if it means my fate is tied to a child."

"He is all yours," Cecil replied. They stepped back, hands up. "Gods know where that human has been. But, Shila, you should be in the room to ensure the human doesn't try to deceive us."

"Who knows," Fanna said, pursing her lips. "You may enjoy the show."

Shila shook her head. She didn't know why it bothered her so much to think of the human with someone she trusted completely, but it did. Maybe because she felt sorry for him. For what her sister had done to his life.

He deserved the chance to make choices of his own right now. She thought of the red vial in her quarters and realized that she could use it as a way to get his support. The vial would reset his life so that none of the past seven years would matter.

"Fine," Shila said after a moment. "We test the product with the human, wait three more days on Atlantis to see if fertilization occurs, and if not, we drop the human off on Earth and call the rest of the rebel troops for a meeting so we can finally take back our country."

And kill that bastard who dared hurt my sister.

Fanna and Cecil nodded. "Okay. Let's go see the human."

Shila and Fanna made their way through the darkness back to the church, while Cecil and the rest of the crew remained to guard the ship. After pushing through the side door and climbing the stairs to the secret alcove on the second level, they found the human sitting crosslegged on the floor between the couch and the bed, bare chested, his skin gleaming with sweat. He was beautiful this way, Shila thought. With his eyes closed, his hands resting gently on his knees, that thin leather strap on one wrist was the only ornament on his body. He took big deep breaths. The muscles of his chest expanded with each inhale and exhale.

"This may be more fun than I thought," Fanna murmured.

"Gods know the last time he's mated," Shila said. "He might be quick."

"Then you'll just have to help finish me off."

When their boots hit the top of the stairs, the human's eyes opened slowly, and the glow of the single bulb illuminated the hard planes of his face.

"You're back," he said. "With another Shukra."

"Fanna," she said. "Second-in-command to our little shipping...business. And you are the human." Shila saw Fanna's eyes darken with interest, her pupils practically swallowing the gold ring around her iris, when the human stood and reached his full height.

Shila stepped closer to him and held up the vial he'd given her. The liquid shined in the overhead light. "Here is how this is going to work. We're going to test your contraceptive. Fanna will take it. Then, in three days, if she isn't pregnant, you will give us the formula, forget that you ever helped my people, and you will get safe passage back to Earth."

Vahman cocked his head. "The yatra already grants me safety. It's your royal duty to help me when I ask for aid. Prita was adamant about that. A trip back to my home planet is not nearly enough of a payment for the cost of my research."

Shila pulled her ace card. "If safety is not enough, then maybe a redo. I was given a serum a few years back by a witch. It will not only take you back to your home planet, but it can return you to the same space and time that you were taken from. You can start over without interrupting the time continuum."

Vahman's eyes bulged as he looked down at the vial

and then back at Shila. "Why haven't you ever used the serum before? You could've changed your own history and saved yourself—"

"I wasn't the witch's favorite customer, so it won't work on me," Shila said, her voice hardening. She didn't add that some things were destined to happen, and she knew her fate would always be the same. "I'll take you back in time and place to your lab safely. It may be a few days before or after, but you'll have your life back. Or what it was seven years ago. *If* this works. Take it or leave it."

Vahman nodded. "My contraceptive works. It should last up to twenty-eight days at peak efficacy."

"We won't be waiting that long to mate," Fanna said, planting her hands on her hips.

"Okay," Vahman replied. "I am happy to supervise and assist in any medical testing before and after you have intercourse with your chosen seeder."

Shila smirked and took one slow step back. She motioned to Fanna. "You'll be doing a lot more than supervising, human. You'll be the seeder that Fanna mates with."

She saw the shock, the surprise on Vahman's face. He looked back and forth between Shila and Fanna.

"*Why?*"

"Because you'll be invested in making sure the contraceptive works," Shila said. "And we also know you'll keep this quiet. I will be in the room to watch, of course. For my crew."

"Being on Shukra for as long as you have," Fanna said, trailing a fingertip down the center of her throat, "I'm sure you've mated with one of our kind before, haven't you?"

Shila knew she had him the moment his gaze darkened

as he watched Fanna's hand. She walked over to one of the discarded chairs, then placed it right behind him, close enough to nudge the back of his knees. She retrieved the second chair and placed it directly in front of him, less than three feet apart, then sat down. Even though there was a bed a few feet away, she didn't want to see them on the sheets, rolling over each other, skin glistening with exertion. No, that was too intimate.

"Fanna?" she called out over her shoulder. "Are you ready?"

"The question is if the human is ready," Fanna said, amusement dripping in her tone.

When Vahman stood frozen in his spot, Shila chuckled. "Come now, Vahman. You enlisted in a sex auction, and you knew there might be consequences. Unless, of course, you are hesitating because your contraceptive doesn't work..."

"I've told you time and time again," he said, his expression hardening. "I have faith in my science."

"Faith and science," Shila said, amused. "Two opposites I've heard before." She slipped the vial out of his limp fingers and held it out to her second. "Fanna? It sounds like our human will participate in our test. Better drink up."

Fanna uncorked the vial and lifted it to her nose for a quick sniff and immediately jerked back. "Gods, that stuff is potent."

"I'm sorry I didn't have time to make it cherry flavored," Vahman said blandly.

"Touchy, touchy," Fanna said. She winked. "Luckily, I like a little bit of sass, and I'm curious enough about mating with a seeder to try it for our people." She closed her eyes, pinched her nose, and tossed back the vial's contents.

"Ugh, that's disgusting," she said, shaking her head, her hair spilling over her shoulders. She tossed the empty vial to Shila. "How long does it take for this thing to work?"

"Between three to five minutes," Vahman answered.

"Good," Fanna said. She winked at Shila. "Just enough time to get you prepared. Take a seat, human. I want to see what I'm working with today."

Vahman's jaw tensed. He looked over at Shila, and their eyes locked. Just like the first time she'd seen him at The Pleasure Chest, Shila was unable to look away from that ridged line around his mouth.

And the heat in his eyes. Was it because of Fanna or because he liked the idea that Shila would be watching him mate?

"Okay, that's long enough," Fanna said. She took a moment to topple the human into the chair. Vahman adjusted himself on the seat while Fanna began stripping. She kicked off her boots and removed her weapons from the waist down. After, she unbuttoned her tunic, leaving it parted to expose the round globes of her breasts barely covered with leather triangles. She left her undergarment where it was, although it did nothing to conceal the plump juicy lips of her cunt.

"Do you like what you see, human?" she whispered as she straddled his lap and scooted forward until they were torso to torso.

Shila watched, her own desire peaking, as Fanna's round ass, tight and firm, was highlighted by the strip of black fabric between her cheeks and over her wide hips. Then Shila had to bite back her groan when Vahman's large hands curved over Fanna's hips to squeeze those ass cheeks.

"That's it, human," Fanna crooned. Her hips gyrated in a wide circle on Vahman's lap. "We're just getting started."

She slipped off his thighs and got to her knees between his spread legs.

Shila's eyes connected with Vahman's again, locked together by a force impossible to break. He maintained their connection even as he lifted his hips for Fanna to slide his slacks down his thighs and passed his knees.

Over Fanna's head, Shila could see the long thick cock Fanna had begun to stroke to full mast. My stars, how Shila craved the feeling of a cock in her mouth, in her cunt. What would it feel like to taste the soft, hard mast? And upon the verge of her orgasm, her muscles locking onto that penis, gripping him until she milked him dry of his seed.

She almost nudged Fanna aside to take her place. What she would give to wrap her lips around the bulbus head, to stroke long fingers up and down the shaft, and pump him hard and firm.

Vahman's eyes turned hazy with desire as Fanna sucked long and slow, taking the entire erection in her mouth as far as she could.

This was more intimate than Shila had expected. They were less than a foot apart, the ridged lines of his neck visible from this distance. She grew wet, her nipples tightening into points when Vahman twisted Fanna's hair around his fist and tightened his hold so he could guide her movements as she sucked him deep.

She knew she was playing with fire, but she couldn't stop herself from unhooking her pants and slowly pushing one hand under the waistband, brushing her fingers over the swollen hot pleasure nub. She began rubbing herself in slow, firm circles.

"Enough," Vahman said, his jaw hardening at the sight of Shila touching herself. She wasn't sure if he was talking to her or to Fanna at first. Then he tugged on Fanna's hair until her mouth slipped off his penis, his erection bobbing up and down. "Adequate time has passed for the formula to take effect and prevent any fertilization."

Fanna was still on her knees as she pulled off her leather nipple coverings, baring her breasts. She was ready to mate. Shila could see it in the way she panted, the soft sound familiar from when Fanna had come to Shila's bed asking for release. Fanna cupped her breasts, holding them as an offering to the man in front of her.

"I want you to impale me with your cock," she whispered. "The first I'll ever take into my body. Captain, is it okay if the human fucks me?"

Shila nodded, her fingers still hidden below the waistband of her pants, rubbing her clit, now in slow steady circles. "Face me," she said. "Look at me as he fucks you."

Vahman tracked Shila's movement, and he began breathing harder. He stroked a hand up and down his erection. "You like to watch," he said, his voice gruff and hard.

She nodded.

Fanna got to her feet, then leaning forward, she let her breasts sway inches from Shila's face. "I can help you if you remove your clothes," Fanna whispered.

"Start, Fanna," Shila replied. "We will see how this goes."

Fanna looked over her shoulder at Vahman. "Ready?"

He grunted in reply, and Fanna took her time to back

up onto his lap, one leg on either side of his before she took a seat facing Shila.

Shila barely suppressed a groan of her own when Vahman's hands curved over Fanna's hips, his fingers and the outer curve of his arms the only parts of him visible from where Shila sat. Then he stroked Fanna's abdomen up to her breasts and cupped them. His large hands were barely big enough to cover Fanna's generous tits before he pinched her nipples between his fingertips. They became impossibly more erect, and Shila began to unbutton her own tunic.

"*Yes*," Fanna hissed. She gripped the arms of Shila's chair and yanked her forward until Shila's knees were touching Vahman's. "Now that's better."

Fanna's mouth covered Shila's, their tongues tangling in a hot, deep kiss until Fanna gasped in Shila's mouth and pulled away, breathing heavily.

"The human knows what to do with his hands," she said.

Shila looked down to see Vahman's fingers under the waistband of Fanna's undergarments. His fingers were rubbing her clit nub in the same rhythm as Shila was pleasuring herself.

She glanced over Fanna's shoulder to see the lines of concentration between his brows. He watched Shila's hand, and as she changed rhythm, he did the same to Fanna.

This was too intimate now, too close to feeling as if he was about to penetrate her body. "Take her now," Shila said. "This is not about pleasure but about testing the contraceptive."

Fanna arched her back. "But who says we can't have a

little fun? Are you worried, Shila, that this human is going to fuck me better than you can?"

Shila's brow quirked. She knew Fanna enjoyed taunting and teasing during mating, but she didn't expect her to be like this with the human, too.

"I haven't seen him do much of anything yet," Shila murmured.

She saw his hands freeze, one between Fanna's legs and the other squeezing a breast. The taunt seemed to have triggered something in him, because seconds later, he shoved Fanna forward until her face hovered close to Shila's lap.

"Take off your pants," he said to Shila. "If you are fingering yourself, then don't be a coward about it."

"You risk your life by calling me a coward," Shila said, but she complied, then scooted to the edge of the seat until he could see her cunt in full view.

Fanna rested her hands on Shila's thighs, her hips lifted, and then Fanna let out a sharp shriek as Vahman pulled her down on his erection.

"He's so thick, Captain," Fanna said, shuddering. "He fills me up so good."

Fanna arched her back while she moved forward and back on Vahman's lap, her breasts swaying as he fucked her in slow, deep strokes.

When Vahman groaned, Shila felt it straight in her cunt, and she shivered at the sound.

"Come here," he said, and Fanna was pulled back by her hair, lodging his penis deeper into her body.

They looked magnificent in front of Shila. Fanna was stretched open, her breasts bouncing, her hair wrapped around one of his fists, Vahman's penis sliding in and out of her body. He was lean but strong. His hair curled in disheveled waves around a face that was a study in concentration.

"Do you wish this were you?" Fanna panted. "Do you envy me because you have to watch him mate with me?"

Fanna's taunting only heightened Shila's pleasure and her need for release. In that moment, she *was* envying her second-in-command, filled up with a thick cock.

"Lick her," Vahman said. He shifted in his chair, then pushed Fanna to her knees on the floor. "Stick your tongue in her cunt and fill her up the way I am fucking you," he said hoarsely.

He got to his knees behind Fanna and shoved into her hard this time.

Shila's hands were pushed aside, and Fanna's tongue replaced them. She parted Shila's pussy lips with one long hard stroke of her tongue, teasing the nub. Then her fingers were pumping inside Shila's opening while she sucked, sending shock waves through Shila's body.

Fanna jerked forward as Vahman began to mate with her forcefully, his skin slapping against hers. He reached down and squeezed swaying breast, eliciting another shriek from Fanna, who then concentrated before burying her face in Shila's pussy again to give her more pleasure.

Shila's eyes rolled back as the orgasm rose in her, a cresting wave of sensation that only made Fanna lick and stroke faster with thorough attention.

"Fuck her good, human," Shila panted. "Fuck her good so she can give it to me."

"No, I am the one fucking you, Pirate Queen," he said quietly.

She looked up at him just as he yanked Fanna off her cunt, stopping the cresting orgasm in one quick move. He watched Shila with wide-open eyes as he pulled Fanna back with a hand over her throat and began tongue fucking her mouth. Fanna's lips were wet with Shila's cum, and he didn't hesitate to give her deep, drugging kisses before he shoved her down into Shila's cunt again.

"Make her come," he ordered, and then Shila couldn't think at all as she gave herself to Fanna's administrations. Shila's interior muscles clenched, begging for Vahman, and remaining unsatisfied even as Fanna's fingers teased her into an intense, earth-shattering orgasm that quickly wrapped her in a vise-like grip, pushing her over that pleasure edge into mindlessness. She lay limp in her seat, naked from the waist down, quivering in the aftershocks, when Fanna's mouth and fingers fell away.

Fanna began to scream so loud that Shila was sure anyone in the pews downstairs would hear her or, at the very least, feel the rafters shake from the human's rough fucking.

Her hands gripping the top of Shila's thighs, locking Vahman inside her as only a Shukra breeder could.

"Wh-what's happening—" Vahman said, shuddering as their bodies remained connected.

"A Shukra orgasm, human," Shila said, panting. "Our bodies will vise around your erection, massaging it and holding it in place until the seeder has released all of his cum. It's our body's way to ensure fertilization. Just stay still for a moment longer."

Vahman pulled Fanna up again by her hair until her back arched. All the while, he watched Shila, his intent stare on hers.

"She has a tight cunt," he said to Shila, breathless, holding Fanna as she came down from her orgasm. He then stroked a hand down her belly and began massaging it, as if cultivating the seeds he'd filled her up with. "Is your pussy this tight, Pirate Queen?"

The question was a jarring one, and enough of a trigger to have Shila sitting up in her chair. She gathered her things and dressed. "We are done here. Now we wait for three days."

Fanna was still impaled on his shaft when he asked, "Am I to wait here?"

"I'll have someone send more provisions for you. You may leave if you wish, but do not draw attention to yourself."

"Captain," Fanna said, gasping as she slid to the floor as if her bones had melted from her body. Shila could see Vahman was still half erect; his cum stained the floor between them. "I wish to stay and fuck the human again. Just once more for good measure."

Shila looked at Vahman, who admired Fanna's prone form and then stroked a hand over her naked thigh.

"Fine," Shila said. Jealousy gnawed in her gut as she watched Vahman roll Fanna to her back and spread her legs. Shila turned to leave just as he crawled on top of Fanna and lowered himself into her welcoming embrace. Their lips met when Shila cursed her oath of celibacy before she turned to go.

She wished she could break her oath for this particular human who had such serious eyes and courage to come seek her out, then submit to her demands while never hiding his own intentions. But she'd lost hope in wishes a long time ago, and soon he'd be gone, and she'd have her crew to service her just as it had always been. Contraceptive or not, she would never let another being control her the way her people had been controlled for centuries.

CHAPTER 4

Vahman never thought that the first time he would have intercourse again after his abduction, it would be with a Shukra being. But he'd been so needy, and when he saw the Pirate Queen slip her fingers under the waistband of her pants, he'd wanted to fuck her so hard. Fanna was a willing partner for his needs, and since the Pirate Queen was the one who ordered their mating, he'd complied. But when she'd left the room, there had been something missing when he'd fucked Fanna a second time.

He used the washcloth he'd wet in the small bath in the back of the church apartment to gently wipe the cum from Fanna's thighs and her plump pussy lips. She had a beautiful body, Vahman thought, as he watched her stretch on the hard floor. She was built and thick like so many beings on Shukra who had come down into his lab.

He'd hated them while simultaneously understanding the importance of his research.

It was because of Prita that he'd begun to dismantle his anger. She was the reason for his abduction, but after so many years of knowing her, they'd become close. Like colleagues who had a greater mission beyond their own existence.

Fanna took the washcloth from his hand and finished the job in cleaning herself up. "Human," she said, amused. "Even if your contraceptive doesn't work, I'm glad I took the opportunity to mate with you."

"It works," he grumbled. He was so sure of it that he was willing to sleep with his captors in order to prove it. Not that he hadn't enjoyed the experience.

"I will remember our time together when I am back on our ship."

Vahman didn't mean to ask, but as he watched Fanna get dressed, he couldn't help speaking the question that had plagued his mind since the Pirate Queen had left them. "Do you, ah, mate with the Pirate Queen? It didn't appear like it had been your first time together."

"Sometimes," Fanna said as she fitted the leather straps over her breasts. "The Pirate Queen understands that some crew members, such as me, have needs. She offers to fulfill those needs almost as a duty when we ask. It's safer if we service each other than go out and mate with other beings. Many of us, the captain included, have taken a blood oath to never mate with seeders after what has happened to us or our families."

Vahman nodded. In the brief conversations he'd had with other Shukra beings, he knew that the planet had been ravaged for centuries because of their ability to be impregnated within three days, regardless of cycle. Their gestational period was only six months as well, and because they were generally a race of peaceful people known to prefer intellectual pursuits, they were an easy target.

Motherhood wasn't a defense, either. When the children were born, they were ripped away from their breeder parents. That's why, according to Prita, there were rarely any children on Shukra and why she lost all eleven of her children to her Brihaspathi bastard husband.

In an effort to protect the Shukra, the royal family had made a deal with a waring seeder planet. A deal for protection and peace. A deal that prevented sexual violence against 80% of the population that were Shukra breeders and hadn't immigrated to the planet or married another Shukra being.

Three generations had complied with the deal.

Until the Pirate Queen.

He stood naked and watched as Fanna pulled on her leather pants then reattached her weapons. So the Pirate Queen had also taken an oath. Blood oaths were often their only method of Shukra beings protecting themselves, and even that didn't work if they were raped.

When Fanna was fully dressed, she turned to Vahman and eyed his naked body. "Are you going to bathe?"

He wanted to, but he also didn't want to be vulnerable considering so many people had the code to his rooms. As if she read his mind, Fanna checked her timepiece and motioned to the bath. "If you make it quick, I can stand watch for you. I am also eager to bathe, but I have a crew that can watch my back."

The idea was sound, and after being intimate, there was no reason for Vahman to believe she would want to harm him. With a quick nod, he retrieved his bag and his discarded clothes before walking to the bathroom and closing the door behind him. The small closet space was clean, which surprised him when he'd first used it the night the priest showed him the space. The walls were tiled white marble and the pedestal sink was wide and sat low to accommodate different beings. The glass cabinet above the sink included disposable sanitary products.

Vahman made quick work of brushing his teeth, shaving, and then using the small open alcove shower. The hot water and soap sluiced the sticky sweat of sex. While he finished bathing, he used the sanitation box behind the door to wash and steam his clothes. By the time he was done, they were laundered, and he was able to put on dry linens.

When he stepped out of the bathroom space, he saw Fanna standing over a small wooden crate that was set on a table in front of the couch.

"This all came for you while you were bathing," Fanna said. She lifted a glass bottle and twisted off the cap. "Some fresh water."

"The Pirate Queen?"

Fanna nodded. "She's really soft by nature. She doesn't admit it, but she wants to take care of everyone. Even though she never became the queen she was supposed to be, it's in her blood to be committed to others."

It was in his best interest to stay quiet, but he couldn't hold back his question. "If she takes care of everyone, then why was Prita on her own for so long?"

Fanna's mouth thinned. She took a sip from the water, then recapped it. "Human, you're asking questions about things that you don't understand—"

"Then help me understand," he said, stepping closer to her. "Prita never spoke of her sister, and whenever family came up, she would walk away. She never told me why she was left alone to rule, how she managed to create the labs, and why her sister who has power, never helped her."

"That is a question that only the Pirate Queen can address," Fanna said softly.

Vahman was sick of hearing that answer, but he could tell that Fanna wasn't going to budge. It was obvious that she was loyal. "Then tell me this: why did you join her crew?"

There was a long sigh. "You're familiar with the Intergalactic Congress?"

He remembered learning about the ruling coalition that established basic peace laws across the galaxies. When Vahman had asked Prita why she didn't approach them for help, she said that disputes had to impact more than just her planet and people for them to get involved.

"I've heard of them."

"They have a rule," Fanna said, her expression twisting with disgust. "Every planet has to be governed by its own people. But Shukra had been terrorized for eons by that point, our people been victimized by sex trafficking, our children stolen and sold off."

"If you're going to tell me about the deal with the Brihaspathi, I already know it."

"When the Brihaspathi took over, the darkest of times fell over the Shukra people. Worse than any other planetary partnership in the past, and there had been some bad ones. My mother and my siblings were raped, impregnated, and their children taken from them. I was hidden away until I was old enough to join the rebellion. There are escape plans for our people to be able to slip off the island discreetly. That's when I found the Pirate Queen, and her ship suited me best."

"The rebellion?" Vahman cocked his head. "What rebellion?" He knew that Prita had been working to try to find the contraceptive for years, but he'd never asked if there was any other dissent against the Brihaspathi.

Fanna's lip quirked at his question. She turned to leave. "That's another question for the Pirate Queen," she said. "The front door is unlocked. Just make sure no one sees you leave and enter, otherwise you'll have to answer questions you don't want to, and if Shila has to come and save you, she's not going to like it."

Shila.

Was that the Pirate Queen's name? How had he not heard of it before that moment? It suited her.

"Fanna?" he called out before the being disappeared down the stairs. "Thank you."

"Don't thank me, Vahman," she said. "I am a cog in a machine, and the master of my destiny is a woman who can either destroy or make yours."

With those parting words, she left. The downstairs door opened and closed with a resounding thud.

"Great," he said. When he was alone, he took stock of his room. He hadn't really spent time there since his arrival. The bed had been comfortable enough, but that was all that he'd used. He walked over to the small table in front of the couch and took stock of the provisions that had been delivered. After spotting a small mechanical black device the size of a ladybug on the inside of the crate, he realized that there was a good chance the Pirate Queen left more than food items. He began his search for any devices that could monitor his activities.

Vahman searched in all the places he'd assume a smart Shukra being would plant devices.

The second device after the one he found in the crate was under the couch.

The third was behind the monitor screen.

The fourth was behind the headboard of the bed. Its soft blankets and comforters were deceiving.

There were six more in various locations. He filled a glass of water that had come with his meal and dropped each one into the container before watching it spark, short-circuit, then smoke.

"If you want to know what I'm doing, Pirate Queen," he said aloud, "you should come and see me in person."

After he checked every inch of the room a second time for good measure, he sat down on the plush seating. He was starving, but he'd learned long ago that the food he'd once enjoyed back home was no longer part of his life. As a prisoner, he'd been given bland and tasteless sustenance only to keep him going. Prita would sometimes bring him treats when she could escape to the lab, but the guards couldn't care less. Even though they were also Shukra beings, they were only there because Prita ordered it. They could care less about his research.

As he unpacked the crate, he wondered if the Pirate Queen sent tasteless food as well. He unzipped the largest container made out of an insulated material that kept his meal warm. This was very different from the priest's offerings which had been of the cold sandwich variety.

The opening widened to reveal the fattest hamburger he'd ever seen. His fingers trembled as he carefully peeled back the foil wrapper to expose a glossy seeded bun, two beef patties, lettuce, tomato, onion, cheddar, and bacon. He smelled it, praying this wasn't a trick.

His throat burned, and his eyes watered.

A hamburger. He used to love hamburgers. This would be his first one in seven years.

After a moment's hesitation, he took a bite, groaning at the explosive flavors in his mouth. He began trembling harder, his breath catching, and a tear escaped the corner of his eye.

"Shit," he said, his mouth still full, his voice hoarse. "Shit."

He managed to swallow the first bite, then immediately shoved as much of it into his mouth as he could. Each flavor, each taste was a reminder of what he'd left behind. His parents taking him to McDonald's when he'd aced his high school exams as a middle school student. His father attempting to barbeque on the small grill on their outdoor patio for the Fourth of July.

Vahman wanted all that again. The chances to make new memories with the people he loved. He'd shoved thoughts of them in the back of his mind for so long only because he knew that thinking about them would destroy his will to live and reclaim his life. But now that he was so close to going back, he relished the thought of home.

Vahman had always wanted a family of his own. A place where he belonged. That had been stolen from him, and how he finally had a chance to get it back.

His body began trembling as a stress response, and he knew that the adrenaline spike had worn off after days of being on the run. He was exhausted and coming down from an energy high. He'd been on overdrive trying to find Prita's sister, trying to get help and now he could just take a moment and accept the fact that he was finally free.

He made quick work finishing the rest of his meal, which included, thank the stars, a shit ton of fries, and chocolate for dessert that was wrapped in a container from an Atlantean establishment. Then, after he was finished, he put his garbage in the receptacle close to the bathroom.

He returned to the sitting area, and packed up the rest of the provisions that were supposed to last him a few days. When he moved the crate over, he saw a small tablet that had been stacked underneath.

"What the hell?"

A tablet meant that there was the ability to access or store information. He picked it up, registering the paper-light weight, before he pressed the discreet button on the side to try to switch it on. The device lit up, and a series of symbols scrolled from the bottom to the top of the screen.

"Okay, this might take me a minute," he mused.

It took him closer to three hours to decode the machine and learn how to use the device. Then he attempted to unravel all of the security patches that sent his browsing data to an offsite location which he assumed was the Pirate Queen's ship.

Why had she gifted him a tablet like this? There had to be some ulterior motive. A woman who was as ruthless as Shila, who knew that her sister was suffering by herself and chose to do nothing, didn't provide food, water, and technology without wanting something in return.

His suspicion was confirmed when he unearthed all the tracers and dismantled them, so the tablet was untraceable. "She is a smart one," he mused as he took off the leather strap from his wrist and carefully removed the microchip he'd hidden in the leather. He quickly inserted it into the available port and held his breath.

It only took a moment for all his data to download and appear on the screen.

"Okay," he said with a soft rush. It was all there. He didn't lose his years of research, his countless hours of work, and the reason for his confinement. The smart thing to do was to save the data on the tablet as a second location should something happen to the leather strap.

After a few more minutes, he figured out how to store

the information, then encrypted it so that if anyone used the wrong encryption key, the device would automatically overwrite the data. Now, if something were to happen to him and the chip, the tablet would serve as a protected backup.

He shut down the file and then opened the browser. He'd gotten in the habit of looking up his family and for details about Earth whenever he had access to an information network. After years on Shukra, all his searches were fruitless, and he was sure Atlantis would have the same result. But the act of looking for information was an important part of remembering he was a captive with every intention of going home.

In the browser, he typed in the name of a news network he'd often listened to when working in his lab years ago.

The website popped up on his screen.

"Oh my God," he whispered. It appeared just as when he'd been on Earth.

Did he have access to the Earth's internet network from Atlantis?

He looked around at the sparsely furnished attic. What was this place? This mythical island that connected time, dimension, and space? How could he possibly access a news network back on Earth? It shouldn't make any sense.

Was it playing with his emotions? His dreams? Or was he finally giving in to the madness that came with captivity?

Vahman was trembling again, and this time, the shaking robbed him of his breath. "It could be a trap," he said. "Be careful. Question everything. Trust yourself." Those words were the motto he'd recited for years.

He started with his capture date and worked forward in time.

There had been a hurricane.

And a global pandemic.

The wars were still ongoing but in different parts of the world now.

Poverty. Famine. Recessions.

And then he saw that in the states, Roe v. Wade had been overturned.

"Son of a bitch," he hissed. "Son of a bitch!" His research; had he been able to complete it in his lab back at home, he could have prevented pregnancies from those who weren't ready or didn't want children. Somehow, someway.

He continued to read and began to grieve the time he had lost.

Vahman inhaled the information, rocking with each punch and blow, sitting on the plush couch away from the things he'd left behind seven years before. His heart pounded so hard that it threatened to crack his rib cage. He searched old social media accounts and was able to locate college friends, distant cousins, and classmates. There were marriages and babies. There were career advancements and deaths.

His parents had retired.

They posted his PhD graduation picture on Facebook every year on the anniversary of his disappearance.

They were alone. No one was there to take care of them. Before his abduction, he had started sending them money. They'd done so much for him, that he wanted to use his salary to support them.

When the tears came again, he knew the terrifying pain that crushed his heart would put him at risk of compromising what was left of his mental stability. Spiraling would only destabilize his focus, and he needed to be on guard for whatever could come his way.

He shut down the tablet, then slid it into his tote bag. With one sweeping look around the room, he knew he needed to leave, and take a short walk to clear his head.

Vahman looped the bag over one shoulder, and after a few testing breaths to clear his head, he walked down the stairs. With a quick check to ensure he was alone, he exited the church and stepped out into the night. The town square was still bustling with crowds despite the late hour. Buildings made of a mix of metal and steel were squeezed between clapboard houses no taller than three stories. There were individuals who looked like humans, and then there were a few with hoods covering their heads so their pointed ears and horns were hidden. He'd thought it before, and he was thinking it again now. Atlantis was a strange place, and it would most likely take too much time to unravel how all the dimensions, times, and places converged at this one port town.

Vahman passed The Pleasure Chest he knew now very well after the auction and found himself in front of The Siren's Call. He'd visited once before to ask for The Pirate Queen, but now he was visiting for himself. He looked up at the unassuming building with its brown exterior and tinted windows facing the square. What better place to go to drown his sorrows than a bar?

He pushed the heavy wood panel of the front door and entered a dimly lit space packed with patrons. There were high-top tables along one wall and round tables in the back with clusters of beings. The long wooden bar had a shiny scarred top, indicative of how clean the owner kept the place.

There was an empty stool in the back towards the end

of the bar, and after canvassing the room, ignoring some of the curious onlookers, he took a seat. He was still trying to make sense of the board hanging from the wall when a being of average height, long straight black hair shaved on one side, and pointy ears stopped in front of him.

"Hi, stranger," they said, adjusting their suspenders. "Back again so soon? I still can't help you."

He remembered their first encounter two days before, and how they'd shut up completely when he asked them if they knew the Pirate Queen. "Don't worry," he said easily. "I already found her."

They leaned against the bar, an amused smile on their face. "Did ya now? Well, that's good to hear. What brings you back then?"

"This may seem like a strange question, but do you by any chance have a beer?"

They chuckled. "We have quite a few."

"I haven't had one in seven years," he said. He scrubbed his hands over his face. "I must be dreaming."

"Most people don't say that when they enter my bar."

"Your bar?"

The being nodded, then winked. If Vahman hadn't spent so much time trying to read the people around him, then he would've missed how the easy-going manner masked something incredibly dangerous underneath. "Now that I know you don't have ill intentions towards a friend, I can introduce myself. Name is Seiko. I'm the woman who owns this establishment." She leaned in closer. "Were ya here for the boat races?"

"For the auction, actually," he said.

Seiko's eyebrows shot up. She lowered her voice to a barely audible whisper. "If you don't mind me saying, people bidding at the auction are still tied up right about now," she said.

"It's a bit complicated," Vahman replied. Then he chuckled, the sound rusty and unused. "Let's just say that it was the only way to get Shila's attention, and I'm here on Atlantis for a few more days before I can go home."

Seiko's eyes almost bugged out of her head. "Did you just say *Shila* bid on you? If she got you from the sex auction, then I have no doubt in my mind that it's complicated for you, darling. What is a woman with a celibacy blood oath bidding on a seeder like you?"

Vahman shook his head. He should've been angry that Seiko obviously knew more than she shared when he'd first met her. She could've saved him a lot of time and effort. "My current situation is exactly why I am in desperate need of a beer."

Seiko slapped a hand on the bar, and the friendly tap had a few of the nearby patrons glancing over in curiosity. "Tell you what, food and drink are on the house. You're going to need your strength to deal with whatever she has planned for you."

Seiko walked away before Vahman could ask her what food she had available. If it was Shukra rations, then he'd pass. "I don't think I'm ever going to get used to Atlantis," he said to himself.

Moments later, she returned with a tall pint, the glass opaque and frosty. She slid a plate piled high with what looked like nachos in front of him. "These are our specialty. Eat up, handsome."

"No, it's fine. Really, I—"

"Don't insult the barkeep," she said, cheerfully. "It's a gift from a half elf. Accept it."

An elf. Fascinating. He knew of the concept from Earth,

understood them to be fantastical creatures. But he knew now that his fantasy was Atlantis's reality.

Vahman nodded when he realized there was no changing her mind. "Ah, thank you. I appreciate it."

"You're welcome," she said, then turned towards the opposite end of the bar when someone called her name.

He was afraid of going into shock again like when he tried the burger, and the last thing he wanted to do was bring attention to himself. But the nachos looked magnificent, and he was desperate to drink the beer.

He slid the glass closer, and squeezed his eyes shut after one testing sip. He was so close to going home that he could taste it. He'd have beer again any time he wanted. He just had to make it through the next few days.

Vahman was halfway through his nachos and on his second beer when a familiar woman slid onto the barstool next to him. She folded her arms on the ledge and leaned forward to wave at Seiko.

"She called you, didn't she?" Vahman said.

"She did," the Pirate Queen replied. "What are you up to, human?"

"Vahman," he replied. "My name is Vahman, and if you're going to have a beer with me, I'd prefer if you'd call me by my name."

The deep brown of her eyes with that brilliant gold ring sparkled with secrets. "I will call you whatever—"

"No, you'll call me Vahman," he repeated, his voice hardening.

She watched him for a moment longer, then with one quick move, she snatched a nacho off his plate. "I'll let you get away with speaking to me like that," Shila started, "only for tonight. You took care of Fanna, and for that, I owe you thanks."

CHAPTER 5

Shila's second, Fanna, had returned to the ship sated and well fucked, gloating at how attentive Vahman had been, how considerate he was, and how he'd ensured she received her pleasure first. Shila hated that she'd felt any embers of desire and jealousy. She planned on squashing her confused feelings by focusing on her plan to extract her sister and go after the Brihaspathi.

But her mind kept returning to the human. There was something about him that drew her. After all he'd been through, he should hate her. Hate her people. Not to mention, his years of captivity should have turned him mad. Instead, he seemed almost protective of her sister, and distrustful of her because of her estranged relationship with Prita.

When Seiko called Shila and said he was sitting at her bar, curiosity got the best of her.

"Should I add this on your tab?" Seiko said dryly as she slid a pint in front of Shila.

Shila winked at her. "Darling, you know I'm good for it."

Seiko shook her head, her black hair shimmering as it shifted over her elf ears. "You haven't been good for it since you showed up on this island, but that doesn't stop you."

She rolled her eyes, then pulled out a coin purse from her hip. She handed it to Seiko who immediately pocketed it.

"I always knew you were a pirate, darling," Seiko said. "But never an untrustworthy one. That's why you'll always be welcome."

Shila toasted her before turning back to Vahman. His eyebrow was raised in curiosity. "You've been to Atlantis many times before."

"It's a port city. An interesting one. And I specialize in cargo shipments."

"Mm-hmm," he said. "The legal and illegal variety?"

"You can call it that," she said, amused at the hint of distaste in his tone. If he only knew. Then, because she had nothing to lose, she told him the truth. "I spent the first two years of my exile here."

He leaned back, a look of surprise on his face. "Your sister mentioned that you were exiled but nothing after that...how did you end up on Atlantis?"

The memories were so vivid in her mind even to this day. The betrayal on her mother's face, the way she'd sold her even though she swore she'd never put Shila through what she'd gone through. "I was the one who was set to marry a Brihaspathi heir."

Vahman placed the glass on the bartop with a hard thud. *"What?"*

"Not Prita's husband, but his older brother. He came to

inspect me, then tried to rape me while his family watched and laughed. I had a knife because we were taught at a young age how to protect ourselves. I slit his throat in the throne room."

His blood had sprayed all over the marble floors and the tile. There were screams, weapons drawn, and she was dragged away and thrown into a cage in the basement. It had been so cold. She didn't know how long she stayed there, shivering and alone. Then Prita came.

"Prita exchanged her life for yours, didn't she?" Vahman asked quietly.

Shila nodded. "My sweet, generous, and caring sister, who thought science could free us, was offered up on a plate, and I was shoved into a one-way cruiser to Atlantis to be sold at the sex auction."

This time, Vahman reached out to touch her hand. She let him.

"You never made it to the sex auction," he said, guesting her fate correctly.

"No," Shila replied. "A *ridiculous* priest saved me, and then I joined Remel's security for a while because of my skill with knives. They used to call me Queen for the longest time because that's what I was supposed to be if I hadn't been exiled."

"That's how everyone knows you here?"

Shila looked over at Seiko who in the moment, had glanced in her direction. She had a questioning look on her face. Shila shook her head, and Seiko went back to drawing beers for her customers. "Yes," she finally said, then turned to Vahman. "That is how everyone knows me. The residents on Atlantis that are here full time, that run businesses, have to protect each other. Remel makes sure that we are a priority."

"How did you become a, what did you call it? Cargo transporter."

The knowing expression on his face made her laugh. "Through Remel's security team, I was able to understand the importance of fulfilling the needs of those who would pay anything for comfort and power. I learned about using them, too. Two years after my exile, the boat race came around. The sex auction after that, and I was able to pick out the vacationers with the most wealth. I targeted them. Won my ship in a game of cards. I started transporting for Remel, then for other politicians, and the rest is history. That's how I became the Pirate Queen."

"There are a few more missing pieces," Vahman said. His eyes remained sharply focused on her. "Your crew. Fanna told me that she preferred your ship to the rebellion—"

Shila smiled. How long would it be before the human put all the pieces together? Before he realized that Shila had been the one supplying Prita with the goods needed for her labs? "Fanna said that, did she?"

Vahman shifted in his seat so that his knees bracketed her hips. "Other than the fact that I wasn't aware of a rebellion, why does she prefer your ship?"

This time, Shila didn't appreciate his tone, but at the same time could understand his confusion. She was beginning to learn that he, as a scientist, saw things in black and white. There was right and wrong. Shila preferred to live in the gray. "Do you honestly think I am the first person to kill or even try to kill a captor? I can't speak for the rebellion or the rest of my crew, but I will say that I never judge if a Shukra tries to defend themselves."

He leaned closer, and she could see the darkest shadows in his eyes. The lines around his lips thinned.

"But you judge your sister. And even after you met a witch along the way who gave you the chance to start over, who taught you how to not only transport in space, but also back in time, you never took it."

Shila stiffened. The witch who had given her the skills to jump space and time needed to escape, and after Shila helped her, she'd given Shila an opportunity to make more money than she'd ever thought possible. Of course, Shila had thought about using the time jump ability to go back. But it was too dangerous. She'd never risk hurting her sister with all the unknown variables.

"I told you; it won't work on me," she said vaguely. "You've been in a lab for years, Vahman. When you realize that time is a lot more flexible than you think, you'll come to know my reasons."

"Reasons you won't tell me."

"That's right," Shila said. Then she leaned in close and whispered in his ear, "The truth is right under your nose."

He didn't say anything for a long minute, then turned so that his mouth grazed over the curve of her jaw. "Will you tell me why you became a pirate?"

"No."

"Prita," he said, pulling back. "She kept tabs on you. That's how she knew you'd be the one who could help me get home."

The thought that Prita cared enough to check in on her when she wasn't supposed to try and make contact pained her heart. Shila thought that she was doing her sister a favor by staying away and working solely with the rebellion as a go-between. Now she knew how wrong she'd been. Her poor baby sister. How strong she had to be to last this long.

Shila looked at Vahman's hands and motioned to them

with a nod. "Did Prita also give you those?" The scars were old, but they looked like they had been painful at one time. She'd noticed them the first time he'd touched Fanna.

Vahman looked down, then shook his head. "No. The first six months on Shukra, I was uncooperative. This was from one of my attempts at escaping the underground lab. I tried to break the hinges on the doors, and I almost lost my hands."

"Did your spirit break instead?" she asked. "Is that why you decided to cooperate?"

"Your sister was the reason I cooperated," Vahman said.

Shila felt her spine stiffening. "Did you develop feelings for her, human? Did her role make you feel sorry? There is no need to be. She's stronger than all of us."

Vahman scowled. "It wasn't like that," he said. "She came down to the infirmary they set up for me. It was only the second time we met, and she had bruises on her cheek. That's when I knew we were both prisoners. My best chance of getting out was to work with those who were just as strong as I was and combine forces."

Shila's hands tightened on her pint until her knuckles whitened from the pressure. Despite her complicated feelings of resentment, as well as the years she and her sister had been apart, she knew she was going to take pleasure in killing the man who hurt her.

Shila watched as Seiko put another plate of nachos in front of them, piled just as high as the last. The half elf was a sucker for a lost soul, which is why she and Seiko had bonded so well together when Shila first arrived on Atlantis.

"I'm okay," Vahman started, motioning to the nachos. "I really don't—"

"Don't insult the barkeep," Seiko said in a sing-song voice as she kept walking by to the other end of the bar.

Vahman sighed, then picked up a nacho chip smothered with toppings. "I'm not sure how Tostitos made their way to this magical port city, but I'll take it."

"I have no idea what that is," Shila said.

"It's delicious, and that's all you need to know." Vahman ate more of the nachos in front of him. He looked ravenous, with complete focus as he enjoyed every bite. But that scowl he'd given her remained on his face.

"After I'm gone," he said when a quarter of the plate had been consumed. "Are you going to use the contraceptive to barter for your sister's life?"

He was fixated on Prita. Not that she could blame him. The constant worry about her sister remained like a steady buzz in the back of her mind. But she'd also be lying if she didn't admit that jealousy reared its ugly head. Damn her vow.

"For all that you know about her, you and my sister must've spent quite some time together," Shila said.

He paused before taking another sip of his ale. "We did," he said.

"Is that who tested your contraceptive for you?"

"It was, but if you're asking if I slept with your sister, the answer is no."

"But you did mate in the seven years you were on Shukra," she said. "Right?"

Vahman turned in his seat again until he resumed his position where his legs bracketed her knees. That's when she noticed the tote bag had been tucked at the base of his stool, the same one that held the vials.

"I didn't mate with any Shukra while I was on your former planet," Vahman said. "It was why I was so hungry when Fanna offered herself and why I wanted to fuck you, too."

Damn.

Shila felt the wet heat grow between her thighs, and she squirmed in her seat. "I don't know if Fanna mentioned this to you, so I'll tell you myself. I took a vow of celibacy from breeders. I have no intention of having children of my own."

"Fanna did mention it. But if you want to mate with a seeder in your lifetime, my contraceptive can give you the freedom to do so without consequence."

"I won't trust it until after Fanna takes that pregnancy test the day after tomorrow."

Vahman nodded, his jaw set. He turned back in his seat. "I understand your wariness. Once it's confirmed, and you fulfill your yatra and return me to Earth, do you know how you are going to use it?"

"That is for me to worry about, human—"

"*Vahman.*"

"Vahman," she said with a sigh. "You just think of those nachos that you'll get back on Earth."

Vahman smiled, and for the first time since she met him, Shila could see the charming softness under his razor-sharp exterior. His face transformed, and he was even more deadly handsome than when they'd first met.

"Why did you enter the sex auction?" she found herself asking.

His smile faded. "It was the only way I knew I could get your attention. No one was willing to tell me where you were, but they all seemed so sure that you'd be at the auction. I'm assuming it was for business reasons."

Shila smirked as she picked up her beer. "You seem so certain of that."

"You took an oath."

"A blood oath," she said smoothly. "Against seeders."

That's when she saw the interest spark in his eyes. "Then you do have intercourse."

"I thought that was clear...Vahman."

There was that charming smile again. "The Pleasure Chest is a...strip club?"

"I do not understand what that is," she said, but she could assume by the words and the faint color she spotted in his cheeks that The Pleasure Chest was indeed a strip club.

"It's where people to go watch dancers take off their clothes," Vahman said. His voice dropped an octave. "While I was waiting for you after your win, some of the... ah, contestants and bidders had begun their contractual term."

Shila felt heat begin to pulse between her legs and she shifted on her stool to ease some of the tension. "Haven't you ever been to a...what was it? A strip club? During your time on Earth? I'm sure this is not unusual."

Vahman was already shaking his head. He bit into another nacho chip piled high with toppings. After he finished chewing, he said, "I was too young when I was in school, and too in-charge when I finally began working in my lab."

Because Shila couldn't help herself, she leaned closer to him, their knees brushing. "But you enjoyed it, didn't you?"

Vahman coughed. "I ah, was distracted."

"I enjoy watching."

The embarrassment in his eyes seemed to fade from

one heartbeat to the next. When he looked at her now, she felt the pressure between her legs intensify.

Shila was being careless, was acting in a way that could jeopardize her safety when that was the only thing that had ever mattered. Her life, her ability to support Shukra from afar was the only thing that had mattered all these years. But just a little pleasure couldn't hurt...could it?

She thought of Fanna, of her crewmate who looked so peaceful and sated after Vahman had taken care of her. She wished to be just as relaxed, feel just as pleasured.

"Come on," she said as she got to her feet. If she wasted anymore time then she'd lose her nerve. "Let's go."

"Go where?" he asked even as he drained his beer and stood.

"To the Pleasure Chest."

CHAPTER 6

Vahman followed Shila next door to the Pleasure Chest where they stood in the shadows, waiting for the crowd at the front door to clear before they entered the lobby. After a tense encounter with a minotaur security guard, a being so large in size that Vahman was stunned speechless, Shila spoke to a guard with green horns next to a red curtain to the left of the main theater. Moments later, the guard pulled the red curtain back and escorted Shila and Vahman up a narrow flight of stairs into a hallway with a long stretch of doors every twenty feet. They stopped in front of a door with a symbol that resembled a crown.

The man with the horns spoke in a language that Vahman didn't understand, but he motioned for them to enter. Shila went first and waved her hand towards Vahman as if impatiently telling him to keep up. Once he did as she requested, the green horned guard closed the door without another word, shutting them inside.

Vahman remained quiet as he inspected their surroundings. A large viewing window that overlooked the main stage took up most of the wall while a red velvet-like chaise lounge big enough for two beings was perfectly situated in front of the windows. Shila flipped the lock on the private viewing alcove and removed the black clip from her hair. She pressed a button at the tip and red light flickered on.

A sensor. She was scanning for listening devices. That was smart, he thought. He couldn't concentrate on what she was doing though. When she shook her hair out of her face, the curls fell in a cascade down her back, and the vibrant richness of it was enough to demand all of his attention. How had he not noticed it before? Her curls swayed over her ass, two thick round curves that shifted as she continued to make her way through the room and move the sensor in an easy back and forth motion over the vents, the corners, the chaise. Then she shook her hair out of her face, and pictures of her naked flashed in his mind. Would she do the same thing with those thick, glossy girls if she rode him?

"Clear," she said as she clipped the sensor back in place.

He shifted to hide the tightness in his pants. "Shila, what are we doing here?"

Shila glanced at him over her shoulder as she sat on the plush velvet chaise. "You have never been to one of those strip clubs on Earth, correct? And you asked me why I came to the auction...other than for business reasons, of course. This satisfies your inquiry and my curiosity."

"Curiosity?"

There was that twinkle of mischievousness in her eyes. "I want to know if you like to watch, too."

Just as she said the words, an announcement filtered through the speakers next to the viewing glass.

"The Pleasure Chest is proud to present..."

The words that followed didn't make sense to Vahman. He walked closer to the glass and looked down at the main stage. Two humanoid beings dressed in what looked like black leather pants wheeled out a large round mattress. In the center of the mattress lay a humanoid. They were barely covered in a gauzy blush pink gown, their breasts concealed only by a hint of fabric, their legs bared by slits up the side of their skirt length. Even at this distance, he could see the pointed tips of their ears.

Elf? Possibly.

The humanoid shifted on the bed, the fabric of her dress revealing shadows of bare skin underneath.

"You are in my line of sight," Shila said from behind him. She'd draped an arm along the back of the chaise, and stretched her legs out as if she was trying to get comfortable.

Vahman gave the elf creature on the bed one last glance before walked over to the chaise and sitting on the far end away from the Pirate Queen. He wasn't sure what he was supposed to do, but he knew in that moment that glancing at Shila was not the best option.

The speakers blasted once more with another introduction, and this time, another humanoid wearing leather-like pants strode out onto the main stage. They had a long tail and horns that twisted and curved over their head. More importantly, they carried a whip.

Vahman leaned forward, curious to know what would happen next. Desire seized his body in the time it took to take his next breath when the horned being lashed out with his whip and effectively broke a single clasp between the elf's breasts.

"So you do enjoy watching," Shila purred. Her voice was deep and throaty from the opposite end of the chaise.

"It is fascinating," he said quietly. The horned being lashed out again, and there was an audible gasp from those in the audience standing at the foot of the main stage. Another clasp was broken and the gauzy material covering the elf's breasts parted even further. With one strong wind, her nipples would be uncovered.

"Would you ever consider performing?" Shila asked.

Vahman glanced at her now. Her expression was curious as she continued to lean back against the chaise. "The opportunity has never presented itself," he replied.

"And if it did?"

"Earth logic is…different," Vahman said. "If an opportunity presented itself, there would be ramifications. Public sex is considered a deviancy, and my reputation, my employment could suffer ill-effects."

Shila leaned forward, her wicked grin enchanting. "You haven't been on Earth for some time, human."

No, Vahman thought. No, he hadn't. In all his years on Shukra, he'd also never thought about what benefits existed outside of the life he'd known. What freedoms he'd have that wouldn't be available to him back in his lab in the United States.

He turned back to the show just as the horned creature stepped on the bed, hovering over the elf. His tail, moving with precision, slid up the length of one bare thigh, parting the dress until it exposed a pale creamy skin, and a pussy that was so wet, he could see the shine from their private viewing room.

A thought occurred to him then. He turned to Shila who was now watching the show, her gaze fixed on the exposed elfish skin.

"Do *you* enjoy being watched?"

Shila's head jerked in his direction. There were remnants of that grin on his face. "I do," she said. "Very much."

Curiosity got the better of him. As a scientist, he was fascinated by the mechanics of a complex formula, and Shila was very complex. "How did you know?"

"How did I know that I enjoy being watched?"

"Yes."

Her smile faded, tinged with a moment of sadness. "That damn priest and what he called 'therapy'."

"Therapy?" Vahman balked. The show in front of him was forgotten now. "You had *therapy*?"

"That's what our conversations were called, I suppose," Shila said. "My exile began because the Brihaspati wanted to watch my betrothed rape me. If I have control over a sexual situation, then I can reclaim power from a moment where power was taken from me."

Vahman always thought that he'd hate the Shukra for taking away his life. For taking away the plans he'd had, the future he wanted to build for himself. The family he had always wanted to create that accepted him for who he was. The Brihaspati were the ones who deserved his rage, not the Shukra.

"I imagine you have opportunity on your ship with your crewmates," he blurted out.

Shila's sadness dissipated and was once again replaced with amusement. She rested a knee on the couch so that she was facing him now. "I do not run a veritable Pleasure Chest on my ship, Vahman. We have jobs. Our needs are only satisfied when it interferes with our work."

"Then when was the last time you were watched?"

There was a long pause. "It has been years," she said

quietly. "When I had first come to Atlantis and worked for Remel."

Vahman's blood began to pound in his chest. He made the offer before he could question himself. "I would like to watch you seek your pleasure, Shila."

The air practically crackled between them. He could see Shila's lips part in surprise, the gold around her iris glowing.

There was a loud gasp and a shriek before an echo of moans filtered through the speakers. Vahman glanced to the main stage, and the horned being was thrusting into the elfish woman now. His tail had wrapped her wrists together and held them over her head, while he pounded into her slender body. The round orbs of her breasts bounced with every hard push, and the cries of their passion along with the sound of coupling from the audience in front of the stage was a cacophony of sensation.

"You would watch me, human? And not want to fuck me?"

Vahman couldn't help himself now. His cock ached against the ties of his trousers, but he reached out and brushed a fingertip against Shila's smooth, supple cheek. "Wanting and doing are two separate things. I will still seek pleasure in watching you achieve yours."

There was desire in her eyes, and he knew that she wanted it now as much as he did. "There is someone," she said quietly.

"Call them."

Shila watched him for another moment before she tapped at the screen on her wrist device. Then they sat in silence, watching the horned being fuck the elf until she was sobbing in orgasmic relief.

Moments later, the alcove door opened, and the same tear-drop face being who had escorted him to the church to meet the Pirate Queen entered the room. She silently closed the door and locked it before crossing the alcove to stand in front of Shila. She didn't even acknowledge his presence.

"Yes, mistress," she said, bowing her head.

"Undress," Shila replied. "Quickly."

The being removed her clothes in smooth, efficient movements to reveal a muscled, lean form, and a cunt with a small nub that looked like it vibrated.

"Ray-ten is an omni," Shila said as she got to her feet. She watched Vahman as she began to unbutton her blouse. "She is also a skilled lover."

The silver bald being made a kneeing sound in pleasure. "Thank you, mistress," she said, her voice filled with reverence.

Shila pulled her shirt apart, revealing her breasts. "Will you behave yourself, human, or will I have to stab you to keep you in place?"

Vahman leaned back in the chaise and adjusted himself. "I told you; I won't touch you."

"Why are you doing this?"

"Because you've shown me that I like to watch, too," he said quietly.

Shila kept her eyes on his as she stepped behind Ray-ten and began to caress the lithe body. Her gaze never wavered as she removed the rest of her clothes and dropped to her knees.

Vahman watched as Shila took her pleasure, as that was the only way to describe it. He itched to pull out his cock, to stroke himself as Shila threw her head back in ecstasy.

But she was mesmerizing. Commanding while also giving so much of herself.

Would he trade this moment for time back on Earth? He didn't even know why he asked himself the question, but it disturbed him to realize that he had to think about the answer. That he knew he'd never experience something like this in his lab, in his work, and in the world that he was taken from seven years ago.

As the cries on the main stage began to fade, Shila locked eyes with Vahman as Ray-ten used her tail and her mouth to bring Shila to orgasm one last time. The Pirate Queen was complex and complicated and frustrating. She left her sister and never looked back. Yet here she was, demanding his attention, too.

She was another puzzle, and as a scientist, he had become obsessed with unraveling her mystery.

CHAPTER 7

Ray-ten left as quietly as she'd come. When she closed the door behind her, the alcove descended into silence. Shila was buttoning up her trousers and her shirt while Vahman debated speaking. But what could he say in that moment? What was he supposed to say?

Just as he thought of a glib response to their moment of sexual connection, Shila's wrist device buzzed.

She tapped the screen. "C, what's up?"

There was a deep, breathless voice that responded. "You need to come back to the ship now. We have a problem. It's bad."

The wrist device went dead, and Shila swore. She quickly holstered the last of her knives.

"Go to your rooms," she said to Vahman. "Stay there, and I'll come to you. It's not safe for you to be out in Atlantis without a guide for this long."

"Where are you going?" he asked as he got to his feet.

"I have business."

She was halfway across the room, when he called out again. "Do you think it has anything to do with Shukra?"

The question had her pausing. She slowly spun on her feet, and he could see the indecision on her face.

"I changed my mind," she said. "You're coming with me."

He balked. "To your ship?"

"Yes," she said. "I can't chance leaving you here. This could be a trap, and someone might have found out about your vials."

Vahman didn't waste any time. He rounded the chaise and reached the door to open it for her. "Then let's go."

Vahman wasn't sure why they were on the run, but it couldn't be for good reasons. He felt his anticipation build as he raced after Shila out of the Pleasure Chest. They cut through the square onto the wide walking path next to the vehicle road. From his memory, he knew that the path led to the forest and docking station. A few yards outside of the center of town, darkness consumed them, and they continued using only the light of the two moons in the sky.

When Shila headed towards the tree line instead of where the other interplanetary ships had been docked, where he had first landed when he arrived in Atlantis, he reach out to stop her.

"We aren't going to the docking station?"

"There is a landing pad in the back," Shila said. "Remel gives me free passage to avoid inspection. He knows that I'd never have sirens on board."

"*Sirens?*"

Shila nodded. "Sirens and those with royal blood *do not* get along, so Remel knows that I would never have one on board. The ships that come in are really only inspected for stowaway sirens. They are forbidden on Atlantis."

Before Vahman could asked where her ship was located, he saw the saucer-like spacecraft hidden in the corner of the tree line, barely visible with the naked eye.

"That is...fucking smart," he said as he trailed behind her. There was some sort of reflective coating on it that camouflaged the craft. A person had to be looking at it intently to see anything but foliage.

"Admire my ship later," she snapped, and grabbed his hand to pull them forward. He linked his fingers with hers even as the ramp lowered, and they jumped on. They'd barely made it halfway into the ship when the doors began to close behind them, the ramp retracting, pulling them inside deeper into the underbelly of the craft. Lights flickered on one by one until the cargo bay was illuminated.

Vahman took stock of the space. On one side, there were four double seater escape pod hover crafts. Directly opposite on the other side of the ship, there were empty storage cages. Right in the center was a cylindrical elevator with a single steel door that slid open.

"I need to find out what's going on," Shila said, even as she pulled him into the elevator shaft. He memorized the numbers as she punched them into the key panel.

"I'll stay out of your way," he said. "But do you think you can get me up to speed?"

"It probably has to do with one of my shipments," she said absently. A line had formed between her brows, and the gold rim around her irises glowed.

"Shipments?"

"I am in the transport business."

"We ran because of...of a business deal?" he asked. This woman was definitely different than her sister. It irritated him—no, disappointed him, that with every passing moment, his gut instinct about the Pirate Queen was wrong. She was just another thief.

"I know what that expression means," she said, crossing her arms over her chest. She looked up as if trying to encourage the elevator to move faster. "There's still a lot you don't know and there's too much at stake for me to stop and try to explain myself. More importantly, I don't owe you anything."

"I didn't say anything," Vahman replied.

"You didn't have to." The elevator door opened to reveal a hallway made of steel and glass. She motioned for Vahman to get out. "Walk to the end of the hallway. There is a canteen you can use. Just wait there for me."

She had to be out of her mind if she thought that he was going to leave her side. Instead, he slammed a hand on the release button next to the elevator doors. "I'm coming with you. And I don't think you have a lot of time to argue with me."

He didn't even have time to take a breath when she gripped his tunic and shoved him against the wall. He felt the impact from him to shoulder blade, and the sting from the blow ratcheted up his desire for her. Shila's fire made him feel *alive* for the first time in so long.

"This is my ship and I'll be the one giving the orders, is that clear?"

"Pirate Queen, don't forget for one minute that I'm in this situation because of you and your sister. I'm not here by choice to join your crew. You can give me all the orders you want but I'm going to fight you if I don't agree with you."

An overhead light in the elevator began flashing red. "Captain," Fanna's voice said from over the intercom. "We need you now."

"Gods damnit," she cursed, and shoved at him again. "Stay out of my way, Vahman. I mean it! This is not an underground lab. You'll get yourself and the rest of us killed if you don't cooperate."

"Yes, Captain," he said, and watched again as she punched in another code. The elevator bounced once as it jerked into motion. He counted two more floors before the car stopped and slid open to reveal a room surrounded by windows. There was another Shukra being in the room. This one had short, cropped hair, and wide shoulders, a thick jaw and muscles that could crush a person's neck with one quick twist.

"Why is the scientist here?" they said as they stopped in front of Shila. They pointed a finger at Vahman as if in disgust.

"Would you rather me leave him on Atlantis?" Shila responded.

"Couldn't he have just stayed in the cargo bay or something?"

"Cecil, just tell me what's wrong with the shipment."

"Hear for yourself," Fanna said. She stood behind Cecil at what looked like a comms table in the center of the room and motioned to a holograph. She gave Vahman a saucy wink, then pressed a button on the dashboard in front of her.

"Shila—" The sound cut out repeatedly. There was static echo, then a language that Vahman didn't understand, despite the fluid in his brain that was supposed to be able to translate multiple alien languages after hearing it once.

"Shit," Shila hissed at his side. "Apollo," she called out, then rushed over to stand next to Fanna. She pressed another series of buttons. "Apollo, what's going on with the shipment?"

There was more static, more disruptive airwaves, then the holograph cleared. It was a humanoid being with a fur-like vest and knives in both hands. They were breathing heavy and sweat glistened off their forehead. "Pirate Queen, no one is here to pick up the shipment. I think the Brihaspathi are onto us. We're going to have to evacuate but we need the money to leave. The Gulshans are threatening to kill us if we don't. Or to turn us in to the Brihaspathi."

"Apollo, how long can you hold them?" Shila asked, leaning forward until she was practically touching the holograph. "You know that we need this shipment."

"Not for much longer," Apollo said, glancing from side to side. "We need backup.

The ship shook and the sound of an engine switching on echoed through the room. Cecil was sitting in one of the four chairs, hands covering two orbs protruding from the dashboard in front of them.

"Hold them off for a little bit longer, Apollo. We're coming to get the shipment, and to give over the money."

Apollo looked from left to right. "Hurry!" Then the holograph faded. Vahman had seen nothing like it, nor did he understand why there were so many people invested in this shipment. But he found the nearest chair and sat in it before pulling the strap over his shoulder. Even though he argued with Shila moments before, he actually knew when he had to sit down and shut up, and this was one of those moments.

"Cecil, do you have Apollo's coordinates?" Shila asked as she slid into the chair next to them. "Do I need to pull them for you?"

"No, they're already in the system," Cecil said.

The ship practically bounced, and then there was a moment of weightlessness before Vahman jerked back in his seat.

Fanna pressed an intercom button and her voice echoed through the room. "We're en route to Gulshan. Report to your stations and take your transfer vials now, Shukrans. This is a mission to save the raid from going sour."

There was a series of voices that responded through the dashboard speakers.

"Check."

"You got it, Fanna."

"Do I finally get to shoot someone?"

"If we're saving Apollo, then it's a waste of our time, but I copy."

That had to be the rest of the crew, Vahman realized as he clutched his bag in his hand. The panel next to his chair beeped, and a small compartment popped up revealing a slim vial with vibrant hued liquid in it. The color was the same as the liquid he'd taken to get to Atlantis in the first place.

"Better drink up, Vahman," Shila called out. "Otherwise, your cells will scramble. There is supposed to be some spell, but we've perfected the transfer fluid so just make sure you swallow all of it in one gulp, and it should work."

He didn't need to be told twice. He bit the stopper between his teeth, yanked it out of the top of the vial, and spit it out before tossing back the liquid. It burned, just as it had the first time he'd taken it, and then his skin tingled. The windows surrounding the ship turned black as they entered the atmosphere, then the bright lights of the stars stretched as they went faster than light speed. They were effectively leaving Atlantis, he thought as the ship flew through the air.

"Gulshan is through the wormhole sixteen degrees to the right," Shila said. Vahman watched her as she tracked the stars and patters in front of her then referred to the monitor on the dashboard. He saw it before she spoke again: the grey mass floating amongst the stars as if it was a child's toy left in a pool.

"We're going through *that*?" he blurted out.

"We are," Shila said. "Let's jump in five, four, three, two—"

There was another jerk, and the ship flew into the floating mass. Vahman held his breath as it swallowed them whole. He felt dizzy, his stomach tightening as he gripped the armrests of his chair. Then he focused on the windows and the black sky changed to an explosion of color. Gases and light fused together to create a painting. In the center of the painting there was a small rock formation. No...a planet? The ship jerked, then slowed until they were almost hovering. The color faded and they were swallowed by dark starlit skies again.

Yeah, it was definitely a planet, Vahman thought. The swirls reminded him of pictures of Mars he'd seen as a child. He'd been more interested in cellular biology than astronomy so he didn't have much else to go off of when it came to contextualizing the image.

Shila yanked off her belt and ran to the elevator. "Cecil and Fanna, get me on the ground. I'm going to free Apollo and his team. If you're close enough, then it'll be easy to load the cargo on our ship."

Her eyes met Vahman's and they held. "Don't get into any trouble while I'm gone," she snapped. Then she slipped through the elevator doors. They closed behind her before Vahman could undo his safety harness and follow her.

"Let her do what she has to do," Fanna said, waving him to sit down. "It'll just distract her, and she works best on her own."

"But she has no backup."

"If things get dicey, we'll go down ourselves," Cecil added. "No need for a human to try to muck things up when you don't have any combat training at all."

Vahman wanted to bite back, to remind them that he was the genius in the room, but he was pretty sure that wouldn't help his cause. Instead, he watched as Cecil maneuvered the ship through the atmosphere. As they approached the planet surface, a dry and dusty desert, Vahman could make out half a dozen ships forming a semi-circle.

"Camouflage shields up," Cecil called out. "We're going in." The engines died, and it was as if they were floating like a paper airplane to the ground, except in one, steady flight path behind the semi-circle of ships.

Vahman could now make out three humanoids, a stack of crates, and an army of guards that surrounded the crates.

"This doesn't look good," Fanna said. "Cecil, move behind one of the Emperor's ship. That obnoxious gold one. They'll feel the air from our landing but because that showpiece is so wide, no one will know where it's coming from."

"They'll know," Cecil replied. "We weren't exactly quiet when we came crashing through their atmosphere."

"Humor me anyway," Fanna said.

Cecil did as Fanna requested and gently landed with

minimal disturbance. Vahman watched their hands as they manned the controls and stumbled to the left as the ship hit the ground. Then there was the rumble of the ramp from the lower level.

"Turn on the speakers so we can hear," Cecil said.

Vahman watched the exact dials, the buttons, and the process that Fanna took to comply. He quickly committed them to memory even as the conversation began to filter into the room.

"You're late," a voice said. Vahman stood and walked over to stand next to Fanna so he could get a better look at the group of individuals talking. Now that they were behind the emperor's ship, it was even more difficult to tell who was speaking when.

"I had somewhere to be." Shila's voice was distinct. "We'll give you your money. Let them go and let us take our crates."

"The buyers never showed up themselves," the voice said. The closer Vahman looked, the more he realized that it was a being standing in front of the group of soldiers with weapons.

"I am here, aren't I?" the Pirate Queen responded.

"But you're just one being. And might I say, the ice queen is as beautiful as her reputation claims. Although, you're not a queen, are you? You're just a Shukra on the run."

"Save it," Shila said. Vahman watched as she circled the crates to stand next to the man who looked like the holograph. "We'll take these and be out of your way."

"The Brihaspathi must be very interested in your cargo—"

"Incoming," Cecil shouted as they pointed to the monitor in front of them. "Shit, there are four different spaceships in the atmosphere. We have four minutes before they land. Five if we're lucky. We gotta get out of there."

"They're delaying Shila," Vahman said with his heart in his throat. "They called the Brihaspathi themselves, and your captain has no idea what's coming. "He ran over to the elevator and jumped inside the minute it opened.

"Vahman, wait!" Fanna called out. She dove in after him. "Cecil, get us ready to leave in three minutes!"

The elevator doors slid shut, and after Fanna keyed in a code, the car plummeted to the cargo floor. Vahman gripped the railing, taking deep easy breaths as the elevator came to a stop and the door opened again.

"Stay *here*," Fanna said, and she was running a moment later. Vahman stepped out after her, and watched as she slipped through a side door and down to the ground level.

"Distraction," Vahman said, gasping for air. "They need a distraction."

He ran over to the cages on the side of the ship, and then scanned the panels until he found one that was unlocked. He pulled it open and inside were rows and rows of what looked like missile launchers.

"Whoa!"

A voice shouted from behind him and a Shukra being he didn't recognize called out. They exited a hidden doorway, their large frame ambling towards him.

"Human, what are you doing?"

"Who are you?"

"I'm Reece. I'm the engineer guy, and a member of Shila's crew of Shukra breeder outcasts." He pressed a hand against his chest. "Let me ask you again. "What are you doing?"

"Creating a distraction!" he said, motioning to the missile launchers. "Now are you going to help me or not?"

There was a look of indecision on his face before he charged forward. "Your funeral," he said. He lifted one of the missiles off the wall and handed it to Vahman.

"Thanks," Vahman adjusted it on his shoulder, grunting under the weight, even as he counted down their time in his head. Three minutes.

"Do you know how to use it?"

"No idea."

The man flipped open the panel at the top of the missile and tapped it. "Point, press this button, and brace yourself."

"Great," Vahman said. He stumbled over to the ramp controls to lower it so he could carry it easily to the ground.

Since it was a humanoid planet, luckily, he didn't have to worry about oxygen otherwise he would've been dead by now. After lurching forward into the grey light shining from the planet's sun, he heard shouting, of the argument getting heated, and he knew he had to act fast.

Vahman set the missile down at an angle in the direction of the emperor's gold ship. Then he flipped open the top. "Point, press the button, and brace yourself," he repeated.

Then he pressed the button.

The chamber locked, whined, and heated between his palms. It rumbled, and fire burst from the end, scorching the ground, before a missile shot out of the top opening straight at the ship. It caused an explosion loud enough to shake the ground. The ricochet knocked Vahman back three feet, burning his shoulder in the process.

"Son of a bitch," he hissed as he lay flat on his back. Stars flashed in front of his eyes.

"Move, move, move!"

There was shouting, then more guns, and he managed to roll to his feet without being sick. He saw through the dust and smoke that there was a gaping hole in the side of the gold spaceship in front of him.

"It worked," he said, registering the surprise in his own voice. Then hobbling forward, he windmilled his arms as he tried to propel his body faster towards the Pirate Queen's vessel. Out of the dust, he saw Shila and Fanna carrying two crates each in their hands. A man that he could only assume was Apollo followed with another set of three crates.

"Vahman?" Shila called out, her eyes going so wide that he could see the ring of gold at a distance. "I told you not to cause any trouble!"

"One minute and fifteen seconds until the Brihaspathi are here," he called back. There was cursing then, and more gunshots. Then he was in the cargo bay with the rest of them, the crates sliding across the floor as the ship lurched and Cecil took off, the ramp barely folded inside the holding area.

"Woohoo!" The man named Apollo shouted as he stumbled to his feet. His sandy brown hair was sticking out in disarray, and his clothes were covered in a layer of sweat caked with dust. "The Pirate Queen did it again. And without losing a dime, too."

Vahman bit back the angry retort, the resentment that he felt building up in his gut as he used one of the crates as leverage to get to his feet. He wanted to ask them if it was worth it. If putting everyone's life at risk was enough to get a few crates of whatever contraband they were carrying.

"Apollo, do you think the rest of your crew will get out?" Fanna asked as she brushed herself off.

He nodded, his smile slipping a fraction. "I have faith that they'll be okay. If you're going to Atlantis, I'll tell them to meet me there once I can reinitiate connection. I don't know when we'll be able to get the devices to the labs in Shukra, though."

"Labs in Shukra?" Vahman jerked to attention. He turned to Shila. "What is he talking about."

"Hey, you're the human!" Apollo said, pointing to him. "There is a warrant out for your head, did you know that? Atlantis is probably the safest place to go if I'm being honest. Most of the people there have warrants."

Vahman's heart was racing now. "You said labs in Shukra. What are you talking about?"

Before Shila could interject, Apollo kicked a crate, and the lid slid off revealing beakers, vials, needles, and all of the other lab supplies that he'd used during his time in Shukra. He picked up one of the packets and saw that the label and manufacturing symbols were the same.

"You didn't really think that the Pirate Queen left her sister to fend for herself," Fanna said with amusement. "Did you?"

He turned slowly to look at Shila now, who stood watching him with her hands tucked in the back pockets of her pants.

"You're how the lab gets the equipment it needs," he said.

"The part that keeps us going," Apollo said with a grin. "We would be dead in the water if we weren't fully funded by royalty herself. But if anyone connected our

Pirate Queen to Queen Prita, then it would be hell for both of them. That's why I'm the go-between so no one knows the two!"

"Apollo, you're going to get yourself killed if you keep yapping," Fanna said. She gripped him by the back of the neck and dragged him towards the elevators. "Come on. Let's get you a cold one to drink from the canteen."

"Yes, ma'am," he said, and continued his one-sided conversation until the elevator doors closed.

Shila and Vahman were left standing alone in the cargo bay, the sound of the engines and motors running on high with half a dozen crates between them.

"You could've told me," he said.

Shila shook her head. "For what purpose? You'll be headed back to Earth soon."

"Don't you think I have a right to know that I'm not working with the enemy? I'm working with someone, who in fact, is the reason why there is a contraceptive in the first place?"

"It changes nothing, Vahman," she said. "And your opinion of me doesn't matter."

Vahman didn't stop to think as he crossed to her, fisted a hand in her hair, and yanked her forward to press his lips against hers. She met the kiss with wild tongue and teeth. His mouth devoured hers as he drowned in her taste. She was rich leather and musk, like heartache and redemption all in one package.

When they pulled apart, their noses touching and their hearts racing between them, Vahman cupped her face so that she couldn't look at anyone but him. "It matters," he said. "You could've told me because it *matters*."

Her gold-ring eyes widened, and for a moment he could see the vulnerable insecurity hidden in their depths before they were quickly masked by the hard exterior of the Pirate Queen. "Don't care about me, Vahman. Those who do inevitably get hurt. The only thing that should matter to you is getting back to the life you've always wanted."

Vahman didn't respond. Instead, he let her go, then followed her lead in packing up the crates with the help of Reece who came out of his engine room when he heard the storage cages open. They stacked the crates before taking the elevator back up to the Captain's Dome.

The entire time, Vahman continued to think about Shila's command.

The only thing that should matter to you is getting back to the life you've always wanted.

The scary, absolutely terrifying rebuttal that rang like a persistent bell in the back of his mind was "what if the life he wanted had changed?"

CHAPTER 8

After they docked in Atlantis, Shila asked Apollo to walk Vahman back to the church on his way to The Siren's Call where he was going to reconnect with the rest of his crew.

Vahman didn't fight her, thankfully, otherwise she would've had to get mean and she didn't want to. Not with him.

She watched through the window as the human retreated into the early dawn, and returned her attention to the rebellion team that was supposed to pick up the supplies and deliver them to Shukra. Where had they disappeared? They never let Shila down before.

Fifteen minutes after she began her search, the dashboards buzzed in the Captain's Dome.

"Shila," Cecil called out from across the room. "We're getting an incoming call."

"Who is it?"

Shila heard Cecil's deep intake of breath. "Prita's *husband*, the ruler of the Brihaspathi people, is waiting on the comm for you."

"Shit," she hissed. That meant Prita had said something, either by force or by choice about the rebellion. They had been careful to never create a direct line between each other, but it was obvious who was funding her lab.

"If that son of a bitch hurt her again, or at the worst, if he killed her, I'm going to skin him alive, and hang him out like a pelt for his planet to see before I drain his body of blood and destroy his entire family."

"We'll help," Fanna murmured from her post next to Cecil.

She approached the center of the room, and keyed in the code so the screen could appear with the caller's face. Moments later, the ruling monarch of the Brihaspathi, with his stark-white hair and deep green eyes, stared back at her from the visual. His cruel mouth pursed in distaste.

"Hello, *Pirate Queen*."

"I don't know who that is," Shila responded.

He looked at her with a disgusting smugness now. "Let's not play games. Your reputation precedes you, Shila Devi."

"I don't know why you're calling after all this time."

"I would've called sooner," he said smoothly, "but it took some time to torture the truth out of those traitors who were smuggling goods onto my planet. They're all dead now, thanks to you by the way."

Shila had to bite back a scream. *No, no, no.* She looked up and could see the horror on Cecil and Fanna's faces. The color drained from their cheeks as the thought of their freedom-fighting brethren losing their lives to this monster.

"What do you want?" she said evenly.

"Tsk tsk. What did I tell you about playing games? I am not a man of patience."

He reached off screen, and Shila's heart jumped when she heard a yelp. A woman appeared a second later, gripped by her hair.

Her face was beaten so badly that both of her eyes were swelling, and her nose had dried blood trailing over her mouth and down her neck. There was a chunk of hair missing from the side of her temple, where it had been torn off her head.

"Prita," Shila said with a shudder. "No."

"Don't give him anything," Prita said in their language, gasping for air. The words were barely audible because of the damage done to her jaw. "Save our people from this."

"Shut up, whore," the Brihaspathi ruler said, and shoved her aside. "Now. Where was I?"

There was a crash, and Shila gripped the edge of the comms table so hard that she was sure she was going to break it. "You were about to tell me how much of a coward you are, preying on people weaker than you because you lack the strength to fight someone with real power. Should I remind you about your oldest brother?"

He roared, his anger blazing so hot that he gripped the comms screen on his side as if he was trying to choke Shila. "For that, your sister gets ten more lashings at my hand!"

"Is that what you wanted from me?" Shila taunted. "A reason to abuse a breeder?" She tried to hold back her own anger. "Because I have nothing else for you, despite what Prita said."

A blood vessel burst in his eye. His voice growled with indignation, and she knew she was looking into the face of a terrorist. "You have the scientist and whatever research he's done on this *ridiculous* attempt at a contraceptive." Spittle spewed from his lips. "You dare interfere with the universe's plans? Breeders are *meant* to have children. It is divine. So listen well if you want your sister to live. I will call you with a designated meeting point in exactly twenty-four hours. If at that time you choose not to comply, your sister will die, and the rest of the beings on Shukra will be sold off until there is no one left on this gods-forsaken planet. And if I hear so much as a *whisper* from the galaxy that there is a contraceptive for Shukra breeders, our deal is off. I will hold you personally responsible, and you will know my wrath. Do you understand?"

Shila couldn't speak, couldn't think of what else to say to this monster who threatened her family and the one person who had been a constant through most of her life. So she remained quiet, hating the return of that smugness on the Brihaspathi ruler's face.

"Twenty-four hours to make your decision before I call. Be ready." The comms died, and the room went eerily quiet.

Shila stood frozen, terror seizing her bones. Her sister was going to die. Unless she did something about it, there was no way Prita could survive her husband.

"Captain?" Cecil said, their voice questioning. "What are we going to do?"

"I don't know."

"The crew would follow you back to Shukra if that's what you wanted," Fanna added. "We would fight by your side. You are the rightful monarch."

"Despite the name, I am nobody's Queen," she said quietly. "I need to think. We have twenty-four hours before he calls with the meeting point. I'll be in town until then."

"The exchange?" Cecil asked, a questioning tone in their voice. "You can't really be considering exchanging Vahman for—"

"I said I don't know. Guard the ship."

She spun on her heels and stormed out of the Captain's Dome, through the lower-level cargo area and out into the early morning hours. In the distance, she could see moons glowing in the navy night sky. Whisps of white clouds passed by, casting shadows at her booted feet.

Prita had grown in the ten years since they had last seen each other. Even though her face was broken and bruised, Shila could see in the dull gold circle in her eyes that she was tired, so very tired. While Shila had been off running cargo and living on adrenaline, experiencing true freedom over the past ten years, her sister had the future of their entire race on her shoulders. Granted every moment since her exile, Shila had been working towards helping Shukra, but she was still free. It made her so angry that she wanted to scream. How selfish had she been? How absolutely childish and stubborn to have let her sister sacrifice herself?

Shila didn't realize that she was headed back towards the church until she opened the panel to the second-floor landing and stomped up the stairs.

Vahman was standing shirtless in front of the couch. There was a computer device in his hand and the soft strains of what sounded like music coming from its speakers. He had more water, and there was food in front of him on the small table. How much could the man eat?

"I didn't expect to see you again so soon."

"I had no intention of coming to see you, either," she said. She stood at the top of the staircase. Now that her feet had brought her here, she was unsure of what to do next.

"Well, it can't be for sex, although I enjoyed our last rendezvous, Pirate Queen."

She tried to smile at that, but she couldn't find it in her to feel any humor.

He motioned to the couch. "Why don't you take a seat? We'll watch a movie together. I'm trying to catch up on technology, media and politics, so when I go back to Earth, I can take advantage of all that I've missed."

She cocked her head, having absolutely no idea of what he was talking about. But it sounded like he was willing to distract her, and she was happy to take him up on that offer.

Shila toed off her boots and crossed the room to sit with the human. With Vahman. "Tell me what we are about to watch. I don't normally have time for this kind of foolishness, but I am willing to placate you."

The corner of his mouth quirked, and when he caught her eying his naked chest, he grabbed his discarded tunic and pulled it on to cover all of that exposed skin. It was a good thing, she thought. It was the right move.

"Let me tell you about *Twilight*," he started. "My mother loved that movie for some reason."

"It sounds hideous," Shila said blandly.

Vahman smiled. "It is. But it reminds me of home."

Shila was quiet for a moment before she spoke again. "What was home like?"

"It was...quiet. My parents were supportive even though they never understood me. My friends were the same, but they knew I would surpass them in successes. I was leading a group of scientists twice my age when I was taken."

"And you want to...go back to the quiet?"

"I want to go back to a time period where I have the chance to have a family of my own. Where I can make a difference on Earth."

Shila nodded. She wanted to make a difference, too. But somewhere along the way, she'd made a mistake, and her sister was now bleeding and broken. "Let us watch this…Twilight."

CHAPTER 9

Vahman didn't think the Pirate Queen would want to have long conversations into the morning, but the lighter the sky became, and the quieter the square outside grew, the more Shila was willing to share her secrets.

"You're telling me," she said slowly, "this vampire *sparkles*, and the human chooses to give up her mortality for him? For a disco ball over a hundred years older than her?"

"Yes," Vahman said. "That is correct."

"That sounds awful."

"What's awful," he said, "is the ending for this show I started watching seven years ago called *Game of Thrones*."

"As someone who is intimately familiar with thrones and monarchies, I can personally confirm they are always awful."

He relaxed into the leather of the seat, watching her shift at the opposite end of the couch from him. They'd spent the past few hours enjoying the shows and movies he'd pulled up on the screen, talking about his childhood and hers, as well as the things they used to love but that no longer mattered to them. It was achingly intimate, this casual conversation with a woman who had so many shields up that she had built a fortress around her heart.

Vahman had a flash of an image, of her hand tucked inside the waistband of her pants, her head thrown back as she pleasured herself, then of Shila watching him as he fucked her crewmate on the floor between her spread knees. The last image was of her taking her pleasure in the alcove room. As sexual and personal as that moment was, speaking to her about television shows on a couch was so much more intimate.

"Can I ask you something?" he said.

She hummed. "What is it, human?"

"Vahman," he corrected.

"Vahman," she said, her voice whisky smooth. "Yes, too many stories have passed in the last few hours for us to be anything else to each other."

"Agreed. Now will you tell me what brought you back here to my door?"

There was a long pause, and her body tensed. He'd told her of his research, and she's told him of Shukra children and the card game in which she'd won her ship. Maybe she was willing to tell him the rest because there was an understanding that she wouldn't see him again after much longer.

Why did that thought make him feel so hollow?

"The rebellion squad that was supposed to intercept the goods on Gulshan and take it to Shukra were captured and killed," she said quietly. He watched her swallow. There were shadows in her eyes now.

Vahman sucked in a deep breath. "Shila, I'm so sorry—"

"It's the price we pay," she said simply. "But they didn't have to die. No one has to die."

He didn't respond for a moment, then reached out and grabbed her ankles so that he could shift her legs to drape over his thighs. She stiffened automatically, but when Vahman didn't let her go, she began to relax again.

"I know you still carry the guilt of giving up your Queen-ship," he said as he kneaded her firm muscles. He was fascinated by the soft planes of her face, the curve of her neck in the dim lighting of the room. "Prita once told me you were trained to lead, and she was trained to study and focus on developing her people's economy. Then you were exiled."

She flinched at her sister's name. "The Shukra royal blood is passed down through the breeder lineage. When I became of marriageable age, there was another negotiation. In the Interplanetary Congress's eyes, they saw nothing wrong with the way that Shukra struggled to protect its people." She spat out the word like a curse.

"On the surface it looks like Shukra breeders maintain the power of controlling who they contract with for protection, but in reality, it's all a farce because there is no other way to get money and supplies," Vahman continued.

Shila nodded. "I heard that my mother died a few days after my sister took the crown. She was supposed to go back to her husband's planet, to my father's people, once she abdicated the throne. She would've had to face the sons that she hadn't seen since they were ripped from her arms at birth. She had never left Shukra before, and knowing what she faced, she probably just…gave up. Prita had to deal with the grief of losing her, too."

"Your sister is strong, Shila," Vahman said. "She survived."

Shila shifted so her feet hit the floor and she was able to sit up on the opposite side of the couch. "Tell me, Vahman. What is Shukra like now? I haven't been home in ten years, and I'm sure there must be something happening that is good."

He shook his head. "I don't know."

"You must have—"

"No," he said quietly. "I spent my entire time in the underground lab. I was given lamps that imitated sunlight, pumped with pharmaceuticals to ensure I remained of sound mind, and I was fed on a regimented schedule. The only break in monotony was your sister's visits. I learned yoga to stay at peace."

In retrospect, he didn't know how it had been seven long years. The days had bled together until there was no discerning start and end. The only way he was able to tell time's passing was the computer system that helped him monitor his studies.

"This experience has to have changed you," Shila said. "How will you go back to your home, to the moment when you were taken, and not expect to feel and be a different person? Those around you will be able to tell. You'll have scars that didn't exist before." She motioned to his hands and his shoulders. "You'll look seven years older, and you'll have trauma responses from your captivity."

The possibility of reliving those years that he'd been missing was a gift he never dreamed of. If he chose to go back as he'd originally planned, he'd find a good therapist, work through his trauma in private, and replicate his research for humans in his West Virginia lab. Then he'd retire and live a quiet life traveling and exploring the world he'd left behind. He'd start his family.

Although he found it hard to ever imagine finding someone as vibrant and complex as Shila the Pirate Queen. She was an equation he was beginning to realize he'd never be able to solve. That was why he now knew there was something lonely about his plans, something that didn't feel quite right now. But he'd reckon with that later. The only thing that mattered was that he wasn't held captive again. Never again.

"Can I ask you something?" he said.

"Ask."

"Tell me about your most exciting pirate escapade. I want to know all the details."

She smirked at him. "My, my, Vahman. It sounds like you have a sense of adventure."

"Wouldn't you if you were held captive for seven years?"

"Of course, but remember, someone else's circumstances are often more appealing in conversation than in actuality."

He nodded. "The grass is greener on the other side and all that. I understand."

"I don't know what you mean by 'grass is greener,' but I will tell you that early on in my pirating days, when the start of a small rebellion found me on Atlantis, I joined the annual ship race just to win the pot and give it all to them."

"The more I find out about you, the more interesting you become," he said, smiling. Then he reached out to brush her hair away from her face. She let him, which only confirmed his hypothesis that she was restless and seeking comfort.

"Why are you here, Shila? You could just leave me up here for the rest of the waiting period if you wanted."

He saw the indecisiveness on her face, and she tilted her head ever so slightly towards his hand. He ran a thumb over the sharp curve of her cheekbone.

"After all this time, I guess I'm still worried about my sister."

"Maybe you can take a piece of the formula and share it with her husband to show him you have a bartering tool, and you can give him something in exchange for her safety."

"I think he wants something more than the formula," she said softly. Then she shook her head. "As much as you believe in your science, we have to test out the contraceptive. We will stick with the original plan and wait the full three days before Fanna takes the pregnancy test."

"Okay," he said. He stood with the intention of retrieving more of the bottled water from his provisions box when his shoulder twinged. He winced and rubbed at the spot.

"Vahman? What is it?" Shila got to her feet.

"It's nothing," he said. "When I shot the missile, there was backfire that I wasn't prepared for. I was going to take a hot shower when you arrived."

She stood behind him then lifted his shirt to expose his back and shoulder. He had to grit his teeth to stop from groaning as she stroked a hand over his bruises. "It's big," she said. "I have an idea on how to fix this that works better than a shower. Are you up for an adventure of our own?"

The way she looked so young and mischievous at him had him agreeing before he knew what she was even asking.

"Yes. Wherever you want to go."

"I'll take you to a place that we both probably need.

Since it's so early in the morning, I doubt anyone else will look for us."

"Lead the way," he said.

They left the church in silence and walked side by side behind the town square buildings. They passed The Pleasure Chest and The Siren's Call again, before they circled some parrot shop.

Then they turned left at a sign that read "docks" even though it appeared to be in the opposite direction of the water. Vahman didn't question Shila, though. He'd take whatever trip she was willing to bring him along on.

After another ten minutes, they reached the edge of the grassy fields on the outskirts of town. They were close to the ship docking station now. It looked so different in the early dawn light than it had the night before.

In front of them stretched a towering section of trees that made up a dense, almost impassible forest.

"Never come in here alone," Shila said as they stepped onto one of the worn paths to the left of the landing pads. "There are a few ways to get in and out of Atlantis, and dimension portals in the forest are one of those ways. But you have to know which portal, and you have to understand how they work. If you walk through a portal, you can end up in a place that will immediately lead to your death."

"You don't have to warn me twice," he murmured.

They penetrated the tree line, and the shadows engulfed them until Vahman could only see in a few inches in front of his face. His fingers were entwined with Shila's as they walked under the brush. The confidence radiating off her helped him relax a fraction, even as he remained alert, focusing his other senses so he could spot any potential threats.

Less than one hundred yards from the edge of the tree line, Vahman saw lights shining from behind some boulders.

"Is that where we're going?" he asked quietly, in the hush under the tree canopies.

"It is," Shila responded. She adjusted the straps around her waist that holstered her weapons. Vahman enjoyed the view of her leather pants fitting snugly over her behind as she swaggered to the edge of a grassy bank. It sloped gently into glowing water that sparkled with blue and white lights.

Shila picked up a stone and casually tossed it in the water. A starburst of color trickled out from where the rock made an impact.

"There's bioluminescent algae in the water," he said, grinning like a fool at the sight. "I've never seen it for myself, but I've always been curious about what it looks like in person. I guess it's still dark enough to be visible to the naked eye."

Shila glanced over her shoulder. "You'll soon have time to go on Earth and do all your exploring and witness this on your home planet."

"I will," he said. *But nothing could top this*, he thought. A mythical port with a forest full of portals, and a pool that billowed steam in the warm summer morning? He kicked off his sandals and dipped his feet into the water. It was *hot*. Bioluminescent algae shouldn't be able to live in a hot spring. But then again, by that standard, half-elf bartenders, minotaurs at sex auctions, and a space pirate built like a warrior queen shouldn't exist either.

"This water has healing properties and is good for your shoulder," Shila said. "Let's get in. You'll be good as new." She was already pulling off her blouse, and Vahman could feel himself hardening at the sight of her large breasts. In this isolated section of the woods, she looked magnificent. The sparks of light from the pool accentuated the naked planes of her body as she removed her weapons and clothes.

His response was to set aside his tote bag, which he'd insisted on carrying with them, and stripping out of his own fitted shirt and pants. He watched the curve of Shila's ass, her cheeks thick and round, disappear under the surface of the water as she waded into the hot spring. He didn't waste any time and followed close behind. The stinging heat enveloped his sore muscles, and steam that circled his shoulders as he moved closer to Shila.

She dipped her head under the surface, and when she reemerged, water sluiced off her face, and she turned to look at him over one naked shoulder.

Vahman didn't bother controlling his urge to swim up to her, then wrap her long hair around his fist and hold her head in place for a deep, drugging kiss. She responded right away, her arms wrapping around his neck, her mouth accepting his tongue, sucking and licking with the same slow, thorough attentiveness as him. Then her breasts pressed flush against his chest, and he could feel the hard points of his nipples nestle in his smattering of chest hair.

When he pulled away, he looked down at her naked face, at her hair pushed back, and her eyes hazy with lust. "Perfect," he said.

She smiled, then pushed away from him to swim in a circle.

"Vahman?" she called out.

"Mm-hmm?"

She watched him with a steady gaze, the water barely

covering her tits. "Your experience with Fanna. Would you do it again?"

"No," he said quickly.

"She wasn't good for you?"

Careful. Be honest, but remember Fanna is a member of her chosen family.

He swam over to Shila, then tread water as he stopped inches from her. "You asked me to have sex with her so we could try the contraceptive. But now you're really asking me is if I had a choice between you and Fanna, then no. I wouldn't choose Fanna again. And out of respect for you, if Fanna asked, I would say no. She's not the one I want now, Shila."

Shila's lashes sparkled with droplets of water. She let out a shuddering breath. "I took a vow of celibacy," she said quietly. "I don't want to bring a child into this world where there is no way to protect them."

"And we'll respect that vow," he replied in the same tone. He then backed her up against the bank. "Do you trust me?"

Her eyes went wide, the gold sparkling with desire. "Y-yes."

"Shila, do you *trust* me?"

"Yes."

"We will respect that vow," he said again. Then he gripped her waist, and with one jerky movement, he propped her up on the bank. Her breasts, large and full, glistened from the hot springs water, with nipples tightened to points, were on full display. He reached out to pinch one of those nipples, enjoying the color of Shila's cheeks darkening with desire. He gripped her hips and lifted them to the surface of the water so she lay half on the bank, half floating on the surface of the hot spring.

"V-vahman," she said, her voice breathless. She leaned back on her elbows, her hair cascading around her shoulders.

Her plump, juicy cunt looked mouthwatering, he thought. He draped her thighs on his shoulders. When Shila made eye contact with him, he leaned forward to bury his face between her pussy lips. She shouted, her eyes went wide, and her thighs tightened around his head.

She tasted like the sweetest, most delicious dessert he'd ever had, and after one, long lick of his tongue, feeling the sheer power and strength of her thrusting against his mouth, he was lost. He gripped her thighs to hold them around his ears, pressing them close as he ate her like she was his last meal. He tongue-fucked her, then used his fingers to tease her until she was screaming so loud the trees around them shook, and the water stilled. He could feel the tightness inside her, aching to feel her gripping his dick, holding him, milking him dry. He used one hand to jack off as he drank her up.

Her hands came up to grip his hair, and she almost slid back into the water if he hadn't been anchoring her in place. Then when she let out her final gasp and shuddered from the aftereffects of her orgasm, he finally let her go. She collapsed into his arms, and he wrapped her close, feeling every strong, hard angle of her body fit against his.

"We won't break your vow," Vahman repeated as they floated in the hot, soothing water. "But you may break my heart."

CHAPTER 10

Shila woke fully clothed on the large bed in the attic. The light was waning outside the shuttered window. She shifted to see the occupant on the other side of the mattress. Vahman was also fully dressed, sleeping soundly next to her. They had returned from the hot springs in the late morning and lain next to each other, inches apart.

There was a part of her that wanted him so deeply but knew that it was too much of a risk. But they'd ventured into even more dangerous territory. She spoke to him about her plans, and he told her of the dreams he had. It was a moment away from reality, a moment that she desperately needed as she waited for the Brihaspathi call.

I would take you with me on my next adventure if you didn't have plans of your own.

Shila had just reached out to touch his hair, spiky in all different directions from air drying, when she heard the soft chimes from the lower level.

It was already time for the evening church service.

She had to get back to the ship. More importantly, she

had to stay away from Vahman until Fanna could test for pregnancy. He was a temptation she could not afford. Even if his contraceptive worked, he would still be gone when she fulfilled her yatra.

The church bells hummed again, and this time Shila slipped off the bed and checked her timepiece for any messages.

S: Safe?

C: Yes. Safe?

S: Yes

Cecil was an excellent second mate. They never asked questions and always took their job very seriously. Fanna was just as focused when she was in the Captain's Dome, which was why Shila knew that even if anything happened to Cecil, Fanna could still keep the ship going.

She walked soundlessly to the bathroom to relieve herself before she straightened her clothes and hair. She needed to go to her rooms, to shower and to replace her clothing. Then she had to plan her next steps.

After one last glance at Vahman's taut back, she put on her boots and headed downstairs. Thankfully, the service hadn't begun.

When she turned right at the panel to exit the church, Rowan blocked her path. He wore his signature floral shirt, and brown shorts with sandals.

"Son of a—"

"Church hasn't even started, Shila," he said.

"Good, because I'm not staying."

"Yes, you are."

The priest was one of the biggest thorns in her side. He was constantly trying to give her advice or offer to save her soul even though everyone knew the church and his practice was for the damned. The problem was that he looked so unassuming with his blond hair that fell to his shoulders. How could she kill someone who had no self-preservation?

She tried to sidestep him again. "I have a ship to tend to."

"And precious human cargo upstairs that I am letting you stash for *free*."

She stopped and looked down at him. "Gods damn it, Rowan."

He gave her that smug look that always irritated the hell out of her. "Your payment is to sit in the back row. Come on, Shila. You're a strong, capable woman. Your bravery knows no bounds. You can make it through church."

"Easy for you to say," she muttered. "Will there be *children*?"

Rowan shook his head. "This is strictly an adults-only service. Not a single child in sight. Which is expected for Atlantis if you ask me."

Shila rolled her eyes. "Fine. But I hate you for this."

Rowan waited until she slipped into the seat closet to the aisle in the very back row before he opened the doors. He welcomed every guest, urged them to go sit as close as they could to the stone altar at the front of the hall.

Shila almost got up twice in the time it took for the service to start, and she scared off more than one being from sitting anywhere near her. If she had to deal with Rowan's liturgy, then she'd do it in silence. Rowan tended to talk about the things she didn't want to hear, and she preferred to wrestle with the demons he reminded her of in isolation.

Five minutes later, there were bells, like a curtain of tiny little ringing drops similar to the ones she wore on an anklet as a child. Then Rowan waved for everyone to settle down before he strolled down the aisle and stood in front of the stone alter.

Maybe she could listen for a bit. It was close to dusk, and Rowan may be able to help her clear her head as she worked through a solution for both Vahman and Prita.

Because there was one thing that was certain. There was no way she could sacrifice Vahman. They'd talked until their eyes grew heavy with sleep, and she knew she was giving him too many liberties, sharing too many secrets.

"Today," Rowan started in his whisky-smooth voice, "you may be seeking answers and spiritual guidance from something beyond yourselves or the world you know. Or maybe you're remembering someone from your past and you want to go to them."

That son of a bitch.

He was all the way at the other end of the hall, but she could still tell he was watching her in the last pew.

Between him and Remel, Shila couldn't get any peace when she visited Atlantis. It was like having two older siblings who wouldn't stop nagging her.

She reached into the compartment built into the pew in front of her and removed the small Diya with a clay lotus-shaped base and wick. Using the match that came with it, she lit the wick and held the Diya in the palm of her hand.

If she were a praying kind of Shukra, she would ask the goddesses to guide her way. Because her instinct was to save her sister. But her sister had risked her life for seven years to try to save everyone else. Prita wouldn't want to be rescued at the risk of all the science she'd worked so hard to develop.

Shila had closed her eyes, relaxed against the back of the wooden pew, candle in hand, when she felt it. The call. It was a whisper, and more dangerous than any weapon that had ever threatened her life.

The feeling licked up the center of her back and circled her throat like a tightening collar until she was gasping for air.

Rowan stopped mid-sentence, his head cocked to the side as if he heard the faint sound of music and he was trying to identify where it came from. Then his mouth gaped. The entire church quieted as his eyes widened, and from this distance, Shila could see the priest mouth the words "oh, no."

In every dimension where magic was as real as science, beings had banded together and agreed to follow one rule: sirens were outlawed. Atlantis had adopted the same law because the siren song could control a breeder in any galaxy, especially if the breeder was from a royal lineage.

Shila's cunt grew wet, her nipples tightening into painful points. She slipped the knife out of her boot and held it in her fist. She was caught in the siren song, but she was still aware enough to kill anyone who came near her. That is, if she didn't die first.

Other beings in the church began gasping, writhing in their seats as the siren song ensnared them in an uncontrollable need to mate. The song would never force people into doing what they secretly didn't desire already, but if it wasn't acted upon, then it could be torture.

And for Shila, that meant unbearable pain.

"No," she gasped. The diya dropped to the floor; the flame licked against the stone and snuffed out. "Oh, no."

There was a cry of pleasure, and Shila watched as beings began stripping. They reached for the person next to them or in front of them, pulling at clothes, giving in to their carnal urge to touch, suck, and kiss. A woman straddled a being with horns who had walked in earlier with another woman. She gyrated on his lap while his wife bent over the front of a pew, and another being lifted her skirt from behind.

Rowan was by Shila's side moments later, his eyes clear of the lust that lay like a fog over the church. He kneeled next to her pew. "You have to break your vow," he said quietly.

She pressed her thighs together, the urge to mate so painful that tears pricked her eyes. "No," she gasped, rocking back and forth.

"Yes," he repeated. "Shila, your royal blood means a siren song is going to kill you if you don't act on your instincts."

She hurt, pain shooting through her cunt. She sobbed with need. In the ten years since her exile, she'd never encountered a siren. She'd been careful to avoid places where they might congregate. How could this have happened in the one port city where she was always supposed to be able to take refuge?

The church was filled with a cacophony of passionate sounds from beings who began an absolute fuck fest. Four humans had brought a woman up to the stone altar, stripped her, and poured holy oil over her naked body. In the light filtered through the stained-glass windows, the woman was positioned on her back in offering. She was filled by a long, thick cock into her mouth, another in her anus, and the third in her cunt. She began stroking a fourth in her fist at the same erratic rhythm of her defilement.

Beings were fucking in the pews with abandon now as Rowan took the knife from her clenched fist and sliced the center of her palm.

"Hey! What are you doing?" The sound of Vahman's voice had her looking up at him, tears streaming down her face. He stopped at Rowan's side, ready to push him away.

"She has to break her oath," Rowan said, getting to his feet. He sliced a similar cut down the center of his palm, and his blood ran bluish red. "Luckily, I'm half siren and can break the oath for her."

"Wait, I saw a sign that said sirens are outlawed," Vahman said.

"Male half sirens are inert, and very few people know about me." Rowan turned to Vahman. "That now includes you."

Shila felt like she was going to combust; her breathing grew shallower, and she saw the floaters at the corner of her vision, even as the sound of flesh slapping against flesh and the roar of passionate cries faded into a hollow echo in her ears.

"Vahman," she whispered. "Rowan, it has to be Vahman."

Vahman gaped in shock when he took in the church. He had an erection that tented the front of his jeans and a trickle of sweat at his temple. "I don't know what's going on but tell me what I need to do to help her," he said, his voice wavering.

Rowan pressed his palm to Shila's, blending their blood together. A light sparked between them.

"Unlike the others who are just giving in to their desires, she'll die if she doesn't mate," Rowan said, his voice hard. "She's royalty, and her blood is more susceptible to magic. Take her upstairs and take care of her. Shila, with the power of the goddesses in the nine galaxies, I grant you freedom from your oath to remain celibate of all seeders."

He'd barely finished before Vahman leaned down and picked her up in his arms. He struggled for a moment, as her bone density was heavier than his, then rightened. She looped her arms around his neck, and when her fingertips touched the bare skin at his throat, she preened at the contact.

Oh gods, she thought. She needed to fuck with a painful intensity. She had no choice. She licked at his neck now, unable to stop herself, and he stumbled to the dark corner in the back of the church. She looked over her head to see if anyone was watching before he typed in the code to slide the panel door open.

The church had become an orgy of epic proportions, a mass fucking, and she was desperate to be as defiled as the woman on the altar.

Vahman put her on her feet and closed the panel firmly behind him before he dragged her body up the stairs. His hands were on her now, touching everywhere from her ass to her breasts, to her cloud of black hair.

He shoved her on the bed, and Shila felt the acute pain of fabric touching her oversensitive skin. Her hands trembled as she unhooked her straps, dropping her weapons to the floor in a loud clatter, before she ripped her shirt open at the buttons.

He retrieved his bag from the corner of the room, removed a vial, and yanked the stopper out with his teeth. Vahman climbed on the bed and held her head with one hand. "Drink."

She opened her mouth, and he poured the vile-tasting chemical down her throat. It burned, and she choked but made sure to swallow each and every drop.

He tossed the vial away when it was empty, and the crash echoed through the room.

"Shila, we don't have to—"

"We do," she cried. Her face was still wet with tears. "Vahman."

His jaw hardened when the back of her knuckles brushed over the tent in his pants. "Three minutes," he said, hoarsely. "We need to wait three minutes at least."

She didn't know if she could wait that long before she'd lose her ability to breathe, to think clearly. She reached for Vahman, ready to beg him, to damn everything she'd fought for in this one hazy moment at the mercy of a siren song, when he reached for the waist of her pants and tugged them down her legs.

"I'll take care of you, my queen," he said softly. "Three minutes. Just hold on."

She felt the cool air on her exposed cunt a moment later, her legs free from the confines of her pants and boots. Then he was tugging her tunic off her shoulders and her bra so she was naked on the white sheets, spread in front of him with her head at the foot of his bed.

He shifted her thighs, leaned forward, and draped them over his shoulders.

"Three minutes," she heard him say again, and then

she felt the first long, slow lick. It was instant relief and pleasure intertwined.

"Vahman," she groaned. She squeezed her breasts, her aching nipples, as she felt his palm press against her stomach, holding her in place as he began to feast. He licked her in fast, hard, and strong strokes, focusing on her clit, before he used his second hand to insert his fingers into the tight hole of her pussy.

He curled his fingers up, and she erupted in his mouth. Her head rolled back as she sobbed. She thought she'd imagined the pleasure he'd given her the night before at the hot spring, but it was real. Vahman was real.

Despite her quick release, the agony was building again, chasing her orgasm like the licks of flames chasing the heels of her release.

"M-more," she stuttered, and he gave it to her. Sucking her clit, tongue fucking her with force, then using his fingers to drive her mad. She was on the verge of another orgasm, panting with each lick and stroke, when he pulled back and got to his knees.

His pants hung past his butt, and his long, thick, hard cock sprung out from the clasp of his pants.

"Three minutes is up," he said, his words hard and cutting as he reached behind his shoulder to pull his shirt off over his head. He tossed it aside, adding to the pile on the floor next to the bed. "I'm going to fuck you, Shila. Is that what you want? Do you want my cock deep inside your pussy?"

She was mindless with need, aching for him in the deepest part of her body, craving his touch. When he gripped her ankles and held her legs straight up in the air, parting them so he kneeled between them, Shila closed her eyes to remember the feeling of this moment.

"I want you to look at me," he snapped.

She opened her eyes again on the harsh lines of his face.

"Have you ever had a cock inside this cunt?" he demanded. "Answer me."

She shook her head, unable to speak.

"You're about to," he said, and then with one roll of his hips, he notched his dick in her folds. He spread her legs up and apart impossibly farther and began pushing inside her until the head of his cock had penetrated her. "Say it," he demanded. "Say you want me to fuck your virgin pussy."

"Vahman—"

He started pulling out, and she shrieked, begging him for more dick. "No, no, don't!"

"Then say it!"

"Fuck my virgin pussy!"

He thrust forward until he was seated completely inside her tight, hot, and wet cunt. She felt him fill her until she was practically choking on his cock.

"Oh gods," she shrieked.

Then, using his hold on her legs, he began rocking back and forth. Her globe-like tits bounced with each thrust, and the best Shila could do to stop from being pushed clear off the mattress was to hold on for dear life.

She didn't know how long he fucked her raw, but she reveled in every single moment of it. Soon he was hoisting her up to sit on his thighs and ride him while he sucked on her tits. Then he flipped her onto her belly, pushing her face into the mattress, and pulled her hair as he fucked her on all fours.

Shila came over and over again, locking his penis inside her with her Shukra muscles, until they were fused, with no way of separating until they finished. And when she couldn't move from coming so much, he rolled her onto her back again, lay on top of her, and gave her a deep, drugging kiss that stole the last of her breath.

"I'm about to come," he panted, and his thrusting slowed until she felt every intimate ridge and part of him. She wrapped her tired arms around his neck and welcomed his hot and wet kiss again. Then, as her mind cleared and she smelled the scent of their sticky sweat and cum on the rumpled sheets, felt the planes of his taut back, she spread her legs to accommodate his weight, so they were pelvis to pelvis.

Once, then twice Vahman pushed inside her, and her inner muscles latched onto his penis, milking him until he came in her, jetting hot streams of seed inside her. He buried his face in the nape of her neck and cried out.

"Shila," he said, kissing the soft spot under her ear. Then more softly: "Shila."

"Vahman," she breathed softly. Her eyes drifted closed. "My Vahman."

CHAPTER 11

Vahman felt like he'd run a marathon while simultaneously getting the best sleep of his life. He'd held Shila as she shook in the aftermath in their lovemaking, her eyes resuming their familiar color, her skin cooling as if she was finally coming back from the siren high. He managed to get up and go to the bathroom, where he wet a towel with warm water. He brought it back to Shila's side, and after rolling her on her back, he wiped the remnants of their mating from her red, swollen pussy.

"Mhm."

"Tender?" he asked, looking back up at her face. Her eyes were closed, and she had one arm bent over her head.

"It's perfect," she whispered back, her voice thick with exhaustion.

He smiled, then finished cleaning before pulling the sheet over her body. "Rest," he said quietly, before returning to the bathroom to discard the towel and relieve himself. When he returned, Shila was sitting up with her timepiece in hand. The sheet pooled at her waist. He'd assumed that she'd sleep.

"What is it?"

"I just need to check on my crew. The siren song would've affected them, too, but not as badly. Thank gods."

"Siren song? Is that what that was?"

Shila nodded, tapping at the small digital keypad on her timepiece. "Yes. It's like a spell, but it can't force you to do anything you don't desire already."

"And it affected you the most because of your royal lineage."

She nodded, then glanced at him. "Thank you for saving my life," she said.

"I have to say, I've never been asked to have sex before to save a life, but I can't say I minded it one bit. I just hope you don't have any regrets ending your oath because there was a siren loose on this strange port town."

"Mm-hmm."

He saw the lines from around her mouth and knew reality was setting in about their circumstances. "Shila, the contraceptive works."

"On breeders with royal blood, too?"

"I believe so," he said. Even after they spent an entire night together talking about their lives, she'd avoided discussing the contraceptive, as if that was the one taboo topic that could break the easy intimacy between them. They were two strangers in a port town tied together by mutual connections, and that likely made it safe to share secrets in Shila's eyes. But Vahman wanted her to understand that their destiny didn't have to start and end on Atlantis. He would remember her when he was back in West Virginia, and he wanted her to remember him as well.

He crossed to her side of the bed, and when she looked

up at him, her eyes filled with distrust, he cupped a hand on the back of her neck. "Even if I didn't know you, didn't trust you when we first met, I wouldn't have put you in any danger."

"Vahman—"

Shila's timepiece buzzed, and she stood as she read the message. "I'm sorry, I didn't realize how late it is. I have to get back to the ship. The King of Brihaspathi is supposed to call within an hour."

Vahman was in the process of picking up her clothes. *"What?"*

She took her pants from his hand, sadness in every line of her face. "He found out about my connection with Prita and now he wants to make an exchange. He plans on stopping the contraceptive from getting out."

Vahman felt his blood pumping harder in his body at the thought of that asshole going anywhere near Shila. "You can't negotiate with someone like that—"

"I know," she said, cutting him off. "I still haven't figured out what to do yet, but it won't be working with the Brihaspathi."

"Let me come," he said. He stroked a hand down her arm. "Let me come back to the ship with you so that when your call is over, we can work through a plan together."

He could still see the hesitation on her face, but she nodded. She was finally beginning to trust him.

"Good," Vahman said. "I'll get dressed."

"Okay," she replied. Then her eyes sparkled with humor. "I guess this way, if there is another siren song, I won't be caught without you."

He knew she intended to make a joke, but it rubbed him the wrong way. If he was being practical, he should just accept his role in her life as temporary and move on.

Vahman finished tugging on his shirt and boots before he retrieved his bag with the vials and computer tablet in it. "I'm ready," he said.

"Good." She strapped a knife to her ankle holster and stood.

They walked towards the stairs, and Vahman stopped her with a hand on her shoulder. "Is there anything in here that I should discard? Am I coming back here tonight to sleep? Fanna should be clear to take the test in another twelve hours, so I can stay with you until those results come in..."

"Rowan and Remel can figure out a way to get this space packed up again," Shila said. "I'll owe them."

Vahman didn't question her. With one last look at the attic room, at the place that had been his first taste of freedom in seven years, he followed Shila down the stairs. When they entered the main church hall, it was empty, and the remnants of what had occurred a few hours before were wiped from its pews and walls.

He thought about the priest, Rowan. What a strange being. He greeted people at the docking station, hosted services, and untied blood oaths. More importantly, he and Shila's relationship was strong. He'd been her therapist, but it also looked like he had been her close friend. Good, he thought. Shila deserved to have people in her life who protected and cared for her. She had quietly been trying to care for her people for years.

They walked in silence to the ship, cutting through the square where there were thinner crowds than the night before. When they passed the docking station and moved towards the tree line, Vahman realized that the craft was parked farther back than the night before, hidden in a cove close to the water docks.

"Come on," Shila said as she motioned for him to follow her up the ramp and into her vessel. "Let me show you a little bit more of my ship than what you were able to see yesterday."

"Does it have a name?"

She turned and raised one sharp brow. "No. Only beings with insecurities have to name their ships."

He muffled a laugh. "Understood."

They entered the lower level, passing the familiar storage bays and the panel with weapons. It was still mostly empty save for the four escape pods on the opposite side of the elevator. Shila walked into the tube and waited for him to step inside after her.

The metal panel of the elevator slid shut, and the car glided to the top floor. It slid open to the familiar Captain's Dome.

Fanna and Cecil were both standing around the center comms table, deep in discussion.

"We were just about to come get you," Cecil said when they spotted Shila. They glanced over at Vahman. "We assumed you were occupied though."

Vahman nodded. "Nice to see you, too."

"Hello, old friend," Fanna said with a warm smile. "I hope you took care of our Captain."

His shoulders straightened at the curious expressions that greeted him. "She is fine," he said.

"Hopefully better than fine."

"Fanna," Shila said with a sigh. "Just tell me if you were able to survive the siren song without bringing seeders onto the ship."

"It was difficult," Cecil replied. "But we made it through together. I think we were farther from where the siren was located, so it didn't have as much of an impact on us."

"That's a relief," Shila said. She then motioned to Vahman. "Cecil, can you take Vahman to the kitchens and get him something to eat? Then send him to my rooms." She turned to Vahman. "Take a look around if you'd like, before you get some rest," she said quietly. "I'll come get you when I'm done. I don't want the Brihaspathi to know you're with us, so I'm keeping you out of sight. Then we'll work on a plan once we figure out where the exchange location will be."

Vahman didn't want to argue with her in front of her crew, so he just stepped aside so Cecil could walk past and lead the way out of the Captain's Dome. When he turned to follow, the back of his knuckles brushed against Shila's, and her pinky quickly curled around his index finger, holding for the briefest second, before letting him go.

He followed Cecil into the elevator shaft without a backwards glance. Cecil keyed a three-digit code into the panel; Vahman quickly memorized it along with the other codes to the ship. Just in case.

When the car began its journey down to a lower floor, Cecil leaned back against the elevator wall, arms crossed over their chest, a smile on their mouth. "I guess I'll be the one escorting you around since the Captain seems to have a little bit of a jealous streak when it comes to you."

"Excuse me?"

Cecil replied, "After the Captain came back to the ship, leaving you and Fanna to continue having a good time, she was in a foul mood. I'm assuming you've made up for it by now, but she might get more jealous since you've been intimate."

"She has no reason to be."

"If you say so," Cecil said.

The elevator slowed, but before the panel door could open, Cecil pressed a red button that stopped the car and dimmed the lights. Their eyes turned flinty.

"Human," they said in a tone harder than the friendly welcome they had shared earlier. "That contraceptive better work because there are more lives on the line than you can possibly imagine."

"It works," Vahman replied, gripping the strap of his tote hard. "And I worked with Prita for years. I understand that she's in danger."

"As is the Captain, if she makes a stupid mistake in trying to keep you instead of trading your human ass and your formula for her sister."

"What?"

Cecil's eyes widened. "She didn't tell you."

"No," Vahman said. "All she mentioned was that she was having a call with the king of the Brihaspathi people. That they wanted the formula."

Cecil made a move to turn the elevator car back on, but Vahman got in their way. "Please," he said. "I want to know what's going on."

Cecil looked at the button behind him, then back at Vahman. "Fine," they said. "I'm pretty sure we're not going to be seeing more of you once Fanna takes the pregnancy test tomorrow. It's only a matter of time before the Captain has to tell you herself."

Vahman waited, bracing himself for the worst possible scenario.

"The reason why the heir of Brihaspathi called Shila," Cecil started. "Was to offer an exchange of Prita's life for you and whatever data you have about your contraceptive. He doesn't want anyone to find out about the contraceptive. Wants all evidence of it destroyed. He's calling again today to give Shila the meeting time and location to make the trade-off."

"Is she going to—"

"No," Cecil said. "But my best guess would be that she would've considered it if you hadn't asked for a yatra. She takes her royal vows very seriously, and a broken yatra can damn her for all eternity."

The yatra. That was why Shila hadn't immediately traded his life. Or was it that she felt something for him beyond obligation?

"I've been a member of Shila's crew since the first year she owned this ship," Cecil continued. "I know she's going to try to keep everything and save her sister, which means she's going up against one of the most powerful warrior families in all the nine galaxies. There is a reason why the Intergalactic Congress doesn't do anything to stop them from all the person trafficking they engage in. They are dangerous. And frankly, they haven't done anything that overtly affects the other galaxies."

Vahman felt like his heart was about to burst from his chest. "She's going on a death mission, isn't she?"

"Correct," Cecil said. They remained in their relaxed position on the opposite side of the car, but Vahman could tell out of the corner of his eye that tension bracketed their mouth in fine lines. They weren't happy with the idea either. Vahman could guess Fanna was probably on the same page.

"Come on, let's get you to the canteen—"

"Wait," Vahman said, his mind racing through all the variables, the possible scenarios and outcomes. He was a genius. Regardless of the number of scientists who came and went in the labs where he worked on Shukra, he and

Prita, a fearless queen who risked her own life for her people, were the masterminds behind a contraceptive that could provide freedom to a planet of beings. He had the power to problem solve this situation, too.

He replayed Cecil's confession in his head until something clicked. "Shila told me that the Intergalactic Congress didn't get involved because the rule was that a dispute had to impact more than one planet."

Cecil nodded. "And they're afraid of the Brihaspathi so they won't bend the rules for us."

"The contraceptive," Vahman continued. "We tested it and it's suitable for breeders from all humanoid species. It's an antibodies formula, and I figured out the key to its development. Would the Congress get involved then?"

Three lines formed between Cecil's brows. "They would probably do more than just get involved. They would side with Shukra to stop further trafficking so the science could be shared widely."

That was it, Vahman thought. That was the key. They had to get word out about the contraceptive. Prita's husband knew that he was powerless if others discovered what Vahman and Prita had created, which was why he was hellbent on destroying all traces of the formula.

But in order to share the news, the timing had to be just right. Prita had to be within their grasp, and they had to make the message strong enough to be immediately believable.

Vahman spun on his heels to face Cecil again. "How many people know Shila's backstory? That she was exiled from home and has a vow of celibacy?"

"Everyone," Cecil said immediately. "The Shukra people are considered to be the wisest, the most resilient, but we have never fought against seeders the way Shila has. She is...a legend now. She stood up for us, for everyone and is the only member of the royal family to have ever done so."

"Would they believe the contraceptive would work if they knew she had broken her vow to mate with a seeder? To mate with me?"

Cecil's eyes widened. "Absolutely. But how would you—"

"Leave that up to me," Vahman said. "And I'm going to ask you to keep it from Shila until I have worked out all the details."

"I don't keep secrets from Captain."

"Then please don't say anything until she asks you. And if she does, tell her to speak with me directly."

Cecil watched him with a discerning eye for a moment but then gave an imperceptible nod. "Deal, human. But that's only because what you hold could save my people from abuse and pain."

"I don't think the Shukra breeders understand the power you all wield," he said. "I'm a cog in a machine, but I plan to do my job to help."

Cecil didn't ask him what he meant. They just pressed the button on the elevator, and the lights flickered once then powered up. Seconds later, they were exiting into a wide cafeteria space with one long dining table on the left side and a set of plush couches and a screen on the other.

"The rest of the crew is probably still in their rooms recovering from the siren song. You can have the space to yourself to eat. If you need to go to Shila's rooms, they're on floor three, second door on the left. Her code is—"

Vahman rattled off the code.

Cecil's eyes widened. "How did you know the code to her room?"

He wasn't going to admit he knew it was Prita's birthday. "I'm a scientist," he said simply.

Cecil rolled their eyes and turned to leave. "I'll keep your secret, human, if you keep my girl alive after all this is over."

Then they disappeared through the elevator door and returned to the Captain's Dome.

Vahman took a deep breath. "Okay," he said. First, he'd eat, then he'd develop his argument to convince Shila to make a sex tape with him.

Because watching her fuck was probably the fastest and the most believable way to get the attention from all nine galaxies.

"I hope they have a burger here instead of that bland Shukra prisoner shit I was given," he said, and began to raid the coolers and cabinets.

CHAPTER 12

The Brihaspathi ruler looked smug when his face appeared on the comms screen.

"Were you waiting for my call like a good little girl?"

Shila felt nauseated after hearing his words. "You've interrupted my business negotiations. As I mentioned to you earlier, I don't have what you're looking for."

"Then your sister will die," he said calmly. "And as our eldest is a breeder, I will sell her off, then one by one break up your family. Your people as you know them will no longer exist. Then your little *rebellion* will know my true power."

The threat weighed heavily on her, and she knew there was no way she could allow that to happen. She looked up at Cecil and Fanna, who stayed out of the viewing screen.

"Is he there with you?" The Brihaspathi scum said. "Is that who you keep looking at when you're not giving me your full attention?"

"I told you, I don't—"

"Pirate *Queen*. We both know you're lying. Bring me

the scientist and all the data by tomorrow." His face was grotesque with the evil that lived inside him. Coordinates appeared on a screen a moment later. It was a central point on Shukra. "A moment late, and you will hear of my wrath from whatever hellhole you're hiding in."

If she fulfilled Vahman's yatra and delivered him to the Rahu region, back to Earth, then she could easily make it to the location in time to facilitate a trade-off. "I'll meet with you just to kill you for threatening me, scum."

She watched his face turn molten red with anger. "Bring Prita," was her sign off before she flipped the comms switch to disconnect the call.

"What are you going to do?" Fanna asked quietly.

"They don't know the contraceptive is complete," Shila said. "Vahman kept that information from Prita, too. We can give them partial data. And we'll hope that's enough to secure the trade." She hated negotiating with the bastard, but she knew he'd uphold his part of the bargain. It sounded like he was desperate to keep the information about any contraceptive a secret. After all, if people found out that there was a contraceptive for breeders, his power could be threatened.

"And the scientist?" Cecil pressed. "Prita's husband said they wanted him, too."

Shila swallowed hard. "We'll just have to get Prita out before they realize we're not delivering on that part of the bargain."

"That could cause a war with the Brihaspathi—"

"I'll die for my people after all. Just like my parents wanted me to," she said. "I don't expect anyone on this ship to sacrifice themselves for me and my family. If either of you or any of the crew wants to stay in Atlantis—"

"We take our oaths seriously," Cecil interjected. "We're here with you to the end, Captain."

Fanna nodded. "Until the end."

Shila's heart ached for what could possibly be the very last transport ride she'd ever take. "We leave in one hour."

She reached the elevator when Cecil called her name.

"Trust the scientist," they said. "He may have a solution to all this."

Shila wasn't sure what Vahman would have to offer in this situation, but she nodded at Cecil before leaving the dome.

A few minutes later she walked to her suite and opened the door. She almost expected Vahman to be sitting on one of her couches and watching something on the tablet she'd provided him with, the same way she'd first seen him when she'd come to visit the night before.

Instead, he was standing in the center of her suite, inspecting his surroundings, a look of surprise on his face. He looked so out of place in the cabin decorated with elegant and minimalist furniture. The door to the facilities was on the far right, and along the left was a panel of cabinetry with a keypad lock. There was a horizontal row of tinted viewing windows, and a flat screen in front of the bed.

"I feel like this ship looks so small on the outside, but you've designed it in a way that makes it appear significantly larger inside," he said, turning to face her.

"I was fortunate enough to earn the ship in this condition."

Vahman looked at her with a bland expression as if he knew there was more to the story. Then he stepped forward and cupped her face in his hands. His hold was warm and soothing. When he rested his forehead against hers, she closed her eyes and leaned into him.

"Are you okay?" he whispered.

Shila rubbed her nose against his. "He's going to kill Prita." Her voice shook with fear.

"Is that what he said?"

She hesitated. There was no reason to tell him more than he needed to know. *He's leaving. He's leaving, and he'll take your secrets with you.*

"If I don't do what he says, then yes," she said, then linked her fingers with his.

"Okay, let's think this through—"

"Don't worry yourself over it, Vahman. You're going to go to the Rahu region, and then we'll handle everything with the Brihaspathi on our own."

He looked stunned as he took a step back. "What are you talking about?"

Shila walked over to the wall cabinet, opened the left door, and then bent down to move some of her personal items aside to reveal a small wall safe. She typed in the code, reached inside, and removed a tube filled with crimson red liquid. "Here," she said as she stood. She turned and handed it to Vahman. "Your way out."

"This is the serum for time travel?" he asked, holding it up to the light. "This is what is supposed to get me back in time and space before my abduction without ruining the time continuum?"

"Yes," she said, feeling the slight ache in her heart. "There is a spell that goes with it. We'll get you back on Earth, near your lab location, and you're supposed to swallow the serum and recite the words that accompany it."

"No."

Her eyebrows shot up clear to her hairline. She didn't think she ever heard someone tell her 'no' as definitively as Vahman just did.

"Excuse me?"

"I said no," Vahman replied. He slid the red vial into his bag that he'd left on the couch, then returned to her side. "I'm not going anywhere until we figure out how to get Prita first. She became my friend, Shila. Regardless of what she did and how I resented her, she's trapped. I am a bargaining chip. Let's use me."

"I can't ask you to do that."

"You're not," he said, and linked his fingers with hers. "I'm offering."

"Vahman." Her voice croaked when she said his name this time.

"Shila, there is so much more I want to know about you. There is so much I want to unravel. This is more time for us, too. When do we leave?"

It was against her own best judgment to take him along, but a part of her was selfish enough to want him by her side. "In one hour. Vahman, I don't want—"

"It's okay, Pirate Queen," he said softly. "It's going to be okay. I'm coming with you."

It was selfish of her to want to keep him by her side, but she'd never been the saint her sister was. If she had to spill blood to protect him, too, then she would. "It'll take us some time to get to Shukra. We'll be using the camouflage shield, so it slows us down because of the power draw. I'm going to then go by myself to meet the Brihaspati scum."

"I'll come with—"

"No," she said. "Vahman, I'm not going to the Rahu region and fulfilling your yatra for you first because you asked, and I admittedly want you with me. But if you come to the negotiation table, it puts us all at risk."

"Are you expecting them to honor the deal without trying any tricks? Shila, you're a pirate. You know people use loopholes. By the stars, they're doing the same thing."

"Vahman, that's not your concern anymore—"

This time, he stepped forward, and dug his fingers into the hair at the base of her neck and tugged hard until her head fell back. "No one tells me what to think or feel anymore—not even you, Pirate Queen." It took less than a split second for him to be on his knees. She hovered over him, her eyes glittering.

"And you need to remember that you are a guest on *my* ship, Vahman."

He didn't say anything, his eyes locked with hers, until her grip eased. She helped him back to his feet. Then, in a move uncharacteristically tender for her, she cupped his jaw and pressed a soft kiss against his mouth.

"My sister saved my life," she said. "Then she put you in my path. The debt keeps growing, and I'm going to go save her."

"I have an idea. We need to record us mating, Shila."

The softness was replaced with bewilderment. She stepped back. "*What?*" She had to have misheard him. Why in the world would she record herself mating with Vahman? The exhibitionist in her stood at attention.

"That's why you need me at the negotiation table. I have an idea."

She was about to ask him to explain when an alarm blasted through the room, and the lights began flashing red.

"Captain." Fanna's voice echoed through the intercom. "It looks like Brihaspathi ships landed in the docking station on Atlantis. Remel's guards just gave us the word. They're being processed right now, but they are looking for you."

Shila ran out the door, Vahman hot on her heels as they raced up to the Captain's Dome. They had to get out of Atlantis now.

The boosters had already been activated and the camouflage shield engaged. Cecil and Fanna were strapped into their chairs, and the faces of the other crew members appeared on two screens.

"Cargo is secure?" she called out.

"Yes, Captain," Mayli said.

"We have enough fuel?"

"Yes, Captain," Gabriella replied.

"Is the ramp up and ammunition loaded?"

"Yes, Captain," Reece answered.

"Engage thrusters, and head up and then out towards the left portal, Fanna. The same one we came in through."

"Yes, Captain."

"Cecil? Get the map ready. We're going light speed towards Shukra. We're going home."

"You got it, Captain." Their voice wavered, and the faces of every crew member looked shaken at the thought. They had all been exiled too. They knew the power of those words.

The ship was like a luxury workhorse. The engines were always properly maintained, and whatever extra profit she had went into ensuring it had the latest and greatest mechanics. It would remain quiet until the very last second before they took off. She sat in the captain's chair between Fanna and Cecil. Shila was aware that Vahman took the seat behind her and strapped in. The dashboards began beeping, and the vials popped up from their storage compartments. They all drank so their bodies stayed in one piece during the portal jump.

"How much lead time do we have before they know we've left Atlantis?" Vahman asked, his quiet strength helping to ground her.

"Not much. But hopefully we'll be gone before they find us."

"We've been spotted," Cecil said. They pulled up the security camera on the left side of the ship. Four different beings in black uniforms and with stark-white hair approached them, weapons strapped to their backs and hips.

"Let's get out of here," Shila said, then took control of the gear shift. They were off the ground and in the air before the Brihaspathi people could draw their weapons.

"Incoming!" Reece called out from the comms. "Formation from the rear, sixteen degrees below us."

They had just passed the cloud level when there was a loud boom. Shila acted on instinct and disengaged the boosters.

They dropped out of the sky.

One, two, three, she counted. Then re-engaged gravity boosters. They fell heavily in their seats, and clattering echoed through the Dome.

The ship hovered right below the cloud line, then shot forward before going up again.

"Create the bubble," she said.

"Captain, they're on our six!" Gabriella shouted.

There was a powering-down sound and then white noise.

"We're in the bubble," Fanna said.

"Bubble?" Vahman asked.

"It's how we move light speed through the portals,"

Cecil said. "Gravity drive engaged in five, four, three, two—"

"Go!"

They jerked back in their seats as the ship shot forward. Lights stretched into long streams of light in front of them, and Shila heard Vahman swear. Then everything went dark. A ring appeared, barely wide enough for the ship.

Her heart began pounding as she did quick mathematical equations in her head. They'd make it without being detected if they pumped up the speed.

"Straight ahead. Not a fraction of a measurement off," she said.

She could feel everyone hold their collective breaths as they headed towards Shukra.

CHAPTER 13

Vahman felt...exhilarated. He was itching to take notes, to ask so many questions about travel, the vessel, the way oxygen was generated by the ship itself. His isolation in the lab meant he had been exposed to only a limited amount of information when it came to life beyond his own solar system. He was also fully engrossed in his research regarding the contraceptive that nothing else mattered to him.

But now that he'd spent time on Atlantis, and with Shila, both in the private conversations they'd shared and, in her bed, it was becoming more and more difficult to accept the fact he would have to forget all this information when he went back home. That he'd never know the truth to all his questions.

And that he'd have to forget the woman who was the answer to so many of them.

He began making a mental list so that he could interrogate Shila with all his inquiries in whatever time they had together. She would be patient with him. She *knew* him.

"Captain," Fanna said. "We have nine hours of flight time before we arrive at Shukra."

Everyone took a collective deep breath as the ship seemed to power down and operated on a low-level hum.

"The Brihaspathi think I'm not going to show up tomorrow," Shila said. Vahman could only see the back of her head, but it was clear from her posture that she was pissed. "They must have gotten the information from Prita that Vahman was sent here. They t-tortured it out of her. I'm sure."

"Do you think they'll be able to follow us?" Cecil asked. "I mean, right now we are like sitting ducks floating along." They motioned to the viewing window with the vast blackness in front of them. "Should we try to take an alternate trajectory?"

Shila shook her head. "This is the most direct path. We'll be late if we try a different route, and I don't want to give him another reason to hurt my sister."

Fanna and Cecil nodded.

Shila unbuckled her seat belt then strode right into the elevator. The panel closed behind her leaving Vahman with her two seconds-in-command. They looked at him then motioned to the elevator.

"Oh. Right." He unbuckled then waited for the car to return before getting inside.

"Good luck, human," Cecil and Fanna said from behind him. Instead of the humorous tone he expected, they spoke to him as if they had put all their faith in his ability to help Shila see options other than a death mission.

Vahman waited for the panel to close before he tapped in the quadrants for her floor. When he reached the cabin rooms, he saw Shila in the distance and called after her.

"Wait! Damn it, Shila, just hold on for one minute."

She turned and saw him jogging down the hall after her. "What is it?"

Vahman stopped when he reached her side. "That's it. You're just going to meet the Brihaspathi people tomorrow, deliver the contraceptive, and get your sister out of there? What about the Shukra people? What about the Brihaspathi troops? I'm just guessing based on that little stunt they pulled back near Atlantis, they have more firepower than you do. Bigger ships. They want me, and I told you that they were going to fight you dirty."

She kept walking until she reached her room. She pushed the door open and waited for Vahman to enter first before she followed.

"I keep giving you an out, Vahman," she said as she slammed the door, closing them both inside. "Why aren't you taking it?"

He turned to look at her, tracing the outline of gold in her eyes. "You already know the answer to that, Shila."

"You've lost your mind then," she snapped.

"I have a solution. I was trying to tell you before we were interrupted."

He watched her cock her head, then irritation flooded her face. "You want to record yourself mating with me."

"Yes."

"Is this an Earthling obsession with recording? Something you can take with you back to your home planet? As enjoyable as we are together, how will this help my sister?"

The thought of taking a part of her home with him as a memory was tempting, but he knew there were more things at stake right now. "If everyone knows you broke your oath, the Brihaspati will be pushed into a corner."

Shila paused in the erratic pacing she'd begun to do

across her bedroom floor. She turned to face him, then crossed her arms over her chest. "Explain."

"What to the Brihaspati want more than anything in the world?"

"Offspring to create an army."

"What happens if the Shukra people can't give them offspring?"

"They lose power," Shila said. "They won't be able to negotiate peacefully with the Shukra people, and their attempt at invasion will be seen as a threat by the Intergalactic Congress which can impact other planets."

Vahman stepped closer to her. "And what if the Congress found out about the contraception? What if everyone found out about this contraception?"

Vahman could see the wheels turning in her head, then the awareness brightening in her eyes. He explained how it could be used as a power tactic, a way to draw attention from other members of the Intergalactic Congress to Shukra.

Vahman almost expected Shila to dismiss him again, but she listened, her head cocked at his idea. They would have the tape ready to be distributed on the news channels, and when they went to meet the Brihaspathi royal family to get Prita out, they'd release the tape.

"This is very unorthodox, Vahman," she said. "I'll be putting myself on display for all beings to see."

"And you'll love it," he said. He knew she would.

Her brow twitched. "That's not the point. The Brihaspathi might choose to just kill us all anyway."

"They can try, but from what you've told me, the Intergalactic Congress is not going to let a discovery like this go unnoticed. Not when it impacts all humanoid breeders."

"Okay," she said after a beat. "Okay, it doesn't hurt to have it in our back pockets."

"There is one more thing," Vahman said. He took a step closer to her. "I want to change my yatra."

Her eyes widened. "What do you mean?"

"I want to change my yatra," he repeated.

"What aid are you seeking now?" This time, the irritation was back. "It doesn't work like that. You get one request from the royal family. That's it. I don't even know if I have to fulfill my end of the bargain considering I'm technically exiled."

He approached her now, heart pounding, as he cupped her hands in his. "I'm just changing the request. And you'll go through with it. Because despite your pirate nature, you have a heart."

Her lashes fluttered as her eyes locked with his. Vahman took her hands and pressed the palms flat against his chest.

"I needed to believe that I could go back home, that I could go to the place I had been taken from in order to survive the seven years I lived underground developing the contraceptive. But what I really wanted was just the freedom to make my own choices again. To have a family and feel like I belong. Shila, I don't think I can go back. Now that I've been freed, returning to my lab in West Virginia would be like a different kind of imprisonment. Unless I can erase all the memories of what I've learned, and of the time you and I spent together on Atlantis, I'll never be the same. I'll be just as starved for liberation as I was on Shukra."

He leaned forward and pressed his lips against hers. Shila immediately responded to his touch, pressing closer to him until they were torso to torso. He could feel her heart thumping against his.

"What is your request?" she whispered.

"My request, from the royal heir of Shukra, is to have the freedom to be where you are, Queen. I want to choose to be with you. Let me join your crew. Let me be your royal consort."

She was already shaking her head, and he knew she was on the verge of denying him, so he pressed an index finger against her lips. "You cannot say no to a yatra. You are bound to deliver one if someone asks it of you. I know the rules."

"Why?" she whispered.

"You have the answer," he whispered back, then pressed a kiss to the base of her neck. "Because you matter. Because you are the most exquisite complex equation that I have ever seen and I want to spend a lifetime figuring you out."

Shila turned to walk away from him, to increase the distance, but he couldn't allow that. He tucked his fingers in the front waistband of her pants and tugged her close again. "Let's put on a show," he whispered against her ear. "Then we can work out the mechanics of the rest of the plan. Come lie with me, Queen. Show me how you would fuck in front of the Brihaspathi family, unconcerned with their threats. Then we'll have the option of sharing how good you are to the world."

Passion flared in her eyes. She wanted a good fuck again. That was clear. And maybe, just maybe, after they were done and he was able to help her relax a bit more, she'd understand his need to be with her even though they'd had such a scarce amount of time together. The hours they spent in the hot springs and in the attic of that church were too painfully short.

Vahman waited for her response, running his thumbs over her knuckles, until she gave a nearly imperceptible nod. "I think this is insanity," she said. "But I've shamed my family before, and everyone knows the exiled Queen of Shukra is now in a dangerous transportation business. This could very well get people's attention."

Vahman retrieved his tablet and then set it up on the console table across from the bed. He turned back to look at Shila. "Ready?" he asked.

She nodded.

When the red dot appeared in the corner of the screen, he centered his face in the camera lens and spoke.

"I am Dr. Vahman A. Raj, a human from the Rahu region, a citizen of Earth who was abducted seven years ago from my lab where I was completing a complex antibodies study on contraception in breeder anatomy. I spent the past seven years in a lab on Shukra, where I helped facilitate the development of a revolutionary contraceptive that can work essentially on every humanoid breeder for twenty-eight days. The study has been successful, and today, we're going to prove to all of you how much you can trust the science."

He stepped back so Shila could appear on the left of the screen. Vahman walked to the other side of the bed, then nodded to her. Since this was about her reputation more than his, he wanted her to lead the scene and to decide how much she'd show and what to do.

When he nodded towards her, he saw her eyes focus on his. She looked determined.

"Take off your clothes," she said quietly.

He complied and pulled his tunic over his head. He

then watched as she began tugging off her blouse as well. Then, as if by an unspoken agreement, they crawled onto the bed before meeting in the middle. He was already hard and hot at the sight of her muscled body, her round, thick breasts, and her wide hips. She slid her fingers into his hair at the nape of his neck, then twisted them so his back was to the camera.

She kissed him, with tongue and teeth as her eyes locked with the screen behind him. For that, he grabbed her ass, then slapped it so that one resounding smack echoed in the room.

"Lights to two," she said, and the room dimmed, leaving the perfect halo of overhead recess lighting on the bed so that the camera focused on their nakedness.

He began to touch her in all the tight hot places that he wished he could've enjoyed the first few times they made love. The back of her knees, the top of her thighs, the softness between her shoulder blades. When he'd rushed to take her virgin cunt the first time they'd fucked, it was about desperation.

This was about theater.

He wanted anyone who watching to not only knew he planted his seed deep inside her womb, but that she was taken care of in the best way possible.

Shila pushed him onto the bed and then straddled his abdomen so her ass was in his face. He felt like he'd died and gone to heaven when she scooted back until her sweet cunt, already wet with need, was right in front of his mouth to feast. It was also in perfect view of the camera to see every inch of her.

Just as he hooked his arms around her thighs to adjust her so she could set her pretty pussy lips right on his mouth, she stroked him once, twice, then took the tip of his penis into her mouth. Good God, he was going to combust already.

He licked her, shuddering as he tried to focus on the task at hand while she began to suck his cock hard and deep. Her hands cupped his balls and gently massaged them while her hips rotated. She was already giving an Oscar-worthy performance, and he was breathless from it.

Vahman lifted his head, parted her sweet cunt, and devoured it. He shuddered when she choked on his dick, and when he moved to pull out, she held him in place. He wanted her coming on his face, soaking his mouth until her juice dripped down his chin. And when she finally came, he helped her up so she could face him.

"Show everyone how deep you can now take a cock."

She whipped her hair back so it cascaded over her shoulders to her hips before she crawled to the end of the bed towards the camera.

Yes, he thought. *God, yes*. She sat back on her heels, pinching her nipples anyone watching and jerking off to her beauty, thrusting her breasts out for him to enjoy.

"Pirate Queen, show them what you can do now that you have nothing to hold you back."

"Get ready," she said, her voice rough with emotion. "Because I have no plans of stopping." She once again parted her legs, but this time, she ensured that there was a clear line of sight to where his dick fit into the tight opening of her cunt. Then, on a groan, she slowly lowered herself onto him.

He gripped her hips, helping her ease all the way down until he was firmly lodged in her.

She was panting now, trembling as he filled her up. "Can they see?" she cried as she rocked back and forth.

"Do they see how you can pump me full of your seed at any moment?"

"Yes, rani," he said. "Yes, my Queen." He reached up to fondle her tits, then because she was aching for a bit of pain with the way she tugged at her nipples, he slapped her breasts until they bounced.

"Ride me," he said. "Ride me so they can see how talented you are. That you know how to fuck me good.

She pressed her palms against his abdomen and began rocking her hips up and down, back and forth, getting into a gentle rhythm with her hair tossed back and her knees digging into the mattress on either side of his hips.

"Yeah, fuck me," he called out. "Fuck me hard."

She bounced with even more vigor now, and Vahman could see from his prone position that his dick was visibly entering her tight hot cunt. It was such a perfect sight. Even if he were to find another partner and Shila preferred to never be with him again, he'd always remember this one image, this one moment in his head.

He felt the orgasm pull up his balls and start at his lower back. He didn't want to be on the bottom when he came in her. He wanted everyone knowing he was going to come inside her body and he'd plug her up so she couldn't escape him. And even then, because of the contraceptive, he'd protected her.

Vahman pulled her down to lie over his chest before he rolled so she was on the bottom. He used as much strength as he had to pin her down and piston inside of her. Her legs flailed with each thrust, and her head hung off the edge of the bed, so every expression of pleasure was clearly visible.

"I'm coming," she panted. "I'm coming!" She let out a shriek a moment later, her muscles tightening around him, holding his penis inside as he began to jet streams of semen into her waiting body.

He looked up at the camera as he buried his face between her breasts. He sucked hard against the inside of one so he could leave his mark on the smooth, deep golden brown skin.

"That," he said, gasping for breath as he looked at the recording feed, "is how much faith we have in the efficacy of this contraceptive. It's steeped in human antibodies science. My human antibodies. The Shukra have it. The Brihaspathi are trying to destroy it. You choose which side you'll take."

CHAPTER 14

Shila woke hours later with the acute awareness that today would be the day she died. There was such a slim chance that she was going to make it out alive, so it was better to be prepared for death and be pleasantly surprised, than to experience death and be wrong.

Her plan was to arrive on Shukra and offer the formula with a few tweaks to make it unusable to the Brihaspathi. She'd need help from Vahman for that. Then she could kill the Brihaspathi king, retrieve her sister, and leave. That tape, the plan Vahman had to draw attention from the Intergalactic Congress, was plan B. It was so absurd that it just might work should she find herself in a moment of desperation.

When she rolled over to touch the space next to her on the bed, to touch Vahman, the sheets were cool, as if he'd left her side hours before. Where could he have possibly gone so early? They had so much to talk about that she'd hoped they'd have a moment of privacy. The night before, he'd shut off the recording, and then they'd made love again until she was too tired, too drugged with the sensation of him, to think of anything else.

Assuming he was probably in the canteen, she made quick work of showering and preparing for the meeting with the Brihaspathi. She sharpened her knives and slid them into the holsters at her waist, her thigh, and her ankle. She rarely used the laser gun, but today seemed to be the right time to pull it out and strap it under her arm.

Vahman wanted to stay with her. He wanted to be free to travel with her and her crew. But would they even live long enough for him to experience life with them? She wasn't going to give him up to the Brihaspathi. But Shila wouldn't let that monster abuse her sister any longer, either.

Twenty minutes later when she entered the Captain's Dome, she found Vahman talking quietly with Cecil and Fanna near the comms panel. In front of them was the orange and purple hues of her home planet Shukra. The sight of it was enough to burn her throat.

"What is going on here?" she asked as she tried to tear her eyes away from the glass windows. Vahman looked up at her, and as if he knew what was going through her mind, he crossed the room so he could take her hands in his. He then leaned forward and pressed a soft kiss against her lips.

"You okay?" he whispered.

"I'm better," she said, thinking of how long it had been since she saw Prita.

Ten years.

The day of her exile.

And only other moment when she'd gotten a glimpse of Prita was when she saw her bruised and battered face on the comms with that Brihaspathi scum.

"We have a little bit of time before we have to meet," she said. "What are you doing?"

"We're trying to figure out the best way to reach the Intergalactic Congress," Vahman said. "There isn't exactly a central communication line for them."

"I really don't think that's where we should be spending our time and energy right at this moment," Shila said. She motioned to Shukra, still feeling the soreness, the aching in her chest at being home for so long after her exile. She'd never felt compelled to come to this side of the universe. "We have a lot to do today with falsifying your tests first, and hopefully not getting killed in the process."

"I told you," Vahman said, squeezing her hand. "I don't think the Brihaspathi are going to fight fair, and as a pirate, I figured you'd know better to assume the same thing."

She knew that was the truth as well, but what more of a choice did she have, she thought. "There is too much at stake."

"We should be landing within the next fifteen minutes," Cecil said. They turned back to the monitors, and their eyes furrowed as they focused on their screens. "What the…"

"What is it?" Fanna asked. She worked next to Cecil, and side by side their hands flew over the dashboard.

"You can't just walk in and gut the king of the Brihaspathi," Vahman said blandly. He squeezed her hands. "That's why we're trying to get as many powerful forces as possible to help."

"I don't think you understand how useless the Congress is," Shila said. "We've reached out to them for help countless times."

"But maybe this time they'll help because it'll affect their planets, too," Vahman said patiently.

"Captain?" Cecil called out. "That's strange. So far we are the only ship in the atmosphere. I feel like that's a concern, don't you?"

"It is," Shila said. She walked over to the dash to see the screens and monitors. They were all blank, as if they were traveling through deep space, and not right next to Shukra.

"Do you think something is wrong with our equipment?" Fanna asked.

Cecil shook their head. "No, but something's off..."

"They're planning a sneak attack," Vahman said, his voice hard. "If something feels wrong, it usually is. We should get out of here and get out now."

"We can't do that," Shila said. "And what did I tell you about interfering? It's my ship and I get to call the shots—"

That's when the ship lurched, and the sensors started to go off, beeping and whirring like mad. "What's happening?" Vahman called out.

"We're under attack," Cecil said. "You're right on the money. It looks like the Brihaspathi." Out of the corner of the left screen, a large oval shaped craft moved into view. It was four times the size of Shila's ship, and it looked like it was equipped with external firearms. Just what Shila needed to start her morning.

"Initiate weapons control," Shila said.

Fanna pressed a series of keys on the dash in front of her, then turned to Shila. "I can't. They have us locked in their orbit. They've dug chains into the left and right sides of our ship!"

The ship lurched again, and this time Shila's heart

began to pound. "Trigger the cargo bay escape pods! Get everyone in the cargo bay, now."

Shila shoved Vahman into the elevator first, and then followed closely behind with Fanna and Cecil. They made it down to the cargo bay in seconds and ran towards the corner with the escape pods. The rest of the crew was already there.

The ship lurched and the beeping became erratic. The lights flickered. "Left side of the mountain range, towards the North Cities," Shila said. She remembered that was where the rebellion had often landed or dropped off provisions. Hopefully that would be safe.

"Everyone, get in the pods, now!" she shouted. The ship lurched again and one of the engines sounded like it blew.

Fanna and Cecil slid into the first pod, then a panel on the side of the ship opened for them to slide into before it was sealed, and they could eject into space. The rest of her team did the same, one by one loading up into the pods and hurling into space.

"Get in," Shila said, motioning to the last pod.

"You first," Vahman replied. He held open the glass dome, and because they were running out of time, she didn't argue.

She flicked on all the controls and settled into the seat. When she looked up, Vahman was still standing next to the pod. "What are you waiting for? We have to go!"

He took off the leather strap that he wore around his wrist and slapped it in her hand. "Hold onto this with your life, Shila. Whatever you do, don't lose it. I have to get the tape."

She looked down at the leather strap, then up at

Vahman again. "That tape means nothing! Get in so we can get you to safety—"

"If I don't make it," he said calmly. "You were the best part of this adventure and in another lifetime, I would've fallen in love with you, too."

With strength she didn't know he had, he slammed a hand over the autopilot button and the dome cover of her escape pod locked into place just as he jumped out of the way. She watched him in horror as he backed away from the ship, pressing a kiss to his fingers and waving at her before he turned and ran back to the elevators.

"No!" she screamed. "Vahman, no!"

But the pod was in autopilot, and it lurched forward to the mini launch pad. Then she was hurling into space with only the memory of Vahman in her mind.

Gods damnit, she thought as she wrapped his leather bracelet strap around her wrist and gripped the controls. Gods damnit, now she had to go save his ass.

CHAPTER 15

Vahman ran as fast as he could, first to Shila's rooms to grab his tote bag and the tablet that had the recording on it, then to the Captain's Dome.

"Please hold on for a bit longer," he whispered as the lights flickered again. He needed the ships power to keep running. When he entered the Captain's Dome, he saw that he was being sucked into the bay of the larger Brihaspathi ship. He stood at Cecil's post and followed their exact steps they had shared that morning. First, he loaded the video, then selected the pre-programmed contacts.

"There!" he said and attached the clip to a message that went to every senator in the Intergalactic Congress. The lights flickered again, and the monitor in front of him glitched.

"No, no, no," he chanted as he hit send over and over again. There was more glitching and he prayed that his tape went through. Finally, a green light appeared on the screen indicating confirmation. "Yes!"

He heard the bay doors forcibly opening on the lower levels and initiated one last call. When an older woman appeared on the screen, a white tunic up to her throat, her eyelashes and brows just as stark white, Vahman immediately began to speak.

"Congress maiden, I am calling from the exiled Shila Devi's ship, the being who was to be the Queen of the Shukra people. The Brihaspathi have committed war crimes that will infect the galaxy, and we need your help. They have waged a war—"

Her eyes went wide, then the monitor shut off. There was a pounding on the metal elevator door, and a troop of armed guards stormed in. Vahman held both hands up to indicate that he wasn't armed, and without a word, they gripped him by the back of the neck and confiscated his bag before they lead him out of the room.

He was ushered onto another ship, and cuffed, before landing on Shukra. In the back of his mind, he wondered if Shila was right about the Intergalactic Congress. If there was any hope at all that they would care. He had to hope. But he knew that if they didn't come, Shila would.

He was dragged in front of double doors off the main hall of what he could only assume was the monarch's residence. That's where they produced the tablet he'd had with him, and the vials from his tote bag.

The doors opened to the Shukra royal gathering room. At least that's what he assumed it was. A giant crest similar to the design on the lapel he'd often seen Prita wear hung on drapes behind a set of thrones. Except instead of the willowy scientist with straight hair braided down her back, there was a large figure with white hair, sitting with legs spread. He held a giant wine goblet in one hand and wore a gold chest plate.

How cliché could this fucker be?

"Do we have a translator?" the king shouted.

"I can understand you," Vahman replied.

The room hushed, surprised at his voice.

"Who are you?" Prita's husband said when Vahman was pulled to a stop a few feet from the foot of the throne.

"Dr. Vahman Raj, human from the Rahu region, and the scientist sent in exchange for the royal queen of Shukra, Prita."

The being's eyebrows shot up, and he got to his feet.

Vahman was surprised that he towered over this leader of the Brihaspathi people. The king was like one of those college guys Vahman used to know back on Earth who claimed to be six feet tall but barely hit five foot eight. He looked like he inhaled some sort of steroid treatment to artificially build his muscle mass.

"The exchange isn't for another two hours," he said. "And I was sure someone with the Pirate Queen's reputation wouldn't be so ignorant that she would let you wander her ship. This seems almost too ridiculous, even for her. I should've realized that she was an unworthy adversary."

Spittle ejected from his mouth, barely missing Vahman's face. He remained silent as there wasn't a question to answer.

The Brihaspathi king began to walk around Vahman in a slow and steady stroll. "So now I have the formula in those tiny little vials, the scientist behind it, and my wife, with absolutely no incentive to negotiate. What's to stop me from killing you and Prita now? To quietly excuse your deaths to this waste of a planet and to report to the Congress that there has been an unfortunate passing in the royal house of Shukra?"

He thought of his last conversation with Shila. "The Pirate Queen has compromised the research."

There was another beat of silence, as if he hadn't anticipated that the Pirate Queen would *dare* mess with him.

"Explain yourself!" There was more spittle.

Vahman waited until the being stood in front of him, eyes blazing.

Stall. Stall as long as you can, with as many lies as possible. It will take him time to find the truth.

"The vials in my bag are filled with colored water. I watched her do it. She also erased the research from my tablet. The actual research is on a chip that the Pirate Queen carries with her. Just in case you caught me before she could negotiate with you herself."

The Brihaspathi warrior stepped so close that his foul breath burned Vahman's nostrils. He made a big show of sniffing. "You're telling the truth, aren't you, human?"

"I have no reason to lie," he said in the calmest voice he could.

"Aren't you going to try to cut a deal? To save your life?" He said. "It's the chip I want, not you."

"I doubt any of your...scientists will understand the research enough to put it together again like a puzzle."

The Brihaspathi heir's expression became thunderous. He lifted a hand to slap Vahman across the face, and at the very last moment, Vahman jerked back. The being swung in a full circle and stumbled.

He got to his feet, ready to charge again, when one of the guards from the back of the room called him. "General, something has entered our atmosphere. You're needed in the security room."

"I'll deal with you later," he hissed, then shoved passed Vahman. "The doctor is familiar with the labs. Throw him down there with Prita. They can get to know each other again. And if he touches my whore of a wife, cut off his arms!"

Vahman wasn't afraid at all when facing off against Prita's abuser. He welcomed it, craved the opportunity to knock the being down a peg. But the thought of going back underground was enough to have him drag his feet so the guards had to be rougher with him. They eventually punched him in his kidneys, so he crumpled in pain, the agony shooting up his sides so he was easier to carry.

He didn't want to go down there. He couldn't go down there again.

Breathe in, breathe out. Breathe in, breathe out.

He closed his eyes when they entered the elevator to go to the lower levels then braced himself for seeing the space that had been his only home for years, praying he wasn't going to succumb to the sheer terror of being trapped.

But when the doors opened, Vahman's shock shadowed all his fear. His lab was destroyed. The benches were covered in shards of glass; the equipment had been shot at with what looked like laser fire. The computers were yanked out of their benches, and there were a few single bulbs lighting the way.

One of the two guards turned to the other. "We're needed upstairs. We've been called on deck."

"What about the prisoner?" the other guard said.

"He won't make it out of here alive," they said. "The whore queen has been cooperative, and humans are notoriously useless beings. We'll lock the tube so he's unable to ride it back to the main levels."

"Fine. Let's go."

And just like that, Vahman was alone again in the large lab, his hands tied behind his back, and with zero ability to communicate his location.

He felt the tension on the bindings and knew it was some sort of metal. He began to sweat, his pulse thready as he looked at his prison again, except this time it was an even worse nightmare.

A voice called out. "Is someone there?"

Vahman didn't even know he was racing towards the back of the lab until he'd fallen to his knees in front of the testing room door. It was made of glass with a small opening underneath. Inside, the light burned so bright that it was painful to look at. There was a single bed designed for a doctor's office, with stirrups and a portable waste facility in the corner. Prita stared back at him, beaten and bloody, from her position on the cold tiled floor. Her fingers were bent at odd angles on one hand, and her shoulder had most definitely been dislocated. At least she was not pregnant again.

"Oh my God, Prita, what did he do to you?" Vahman whispered.

Tears pricked her eyes. "What are you doing here? You were supposed to go back to Earth. Did you not find my sister?"

"Let's get you out of there first," he said. He began looking around behind him, searching for something, anything to untie his bindings, to then let her out of there.

"You have the Brihaspathi ties," she said, her mouth barely able to form words. "There is a magnet you can hold in one hand and press to the metal. It then becomes malleable, and you'll be able to pull free."

"Where can I get this magnet?" he asked.

She lifted one trembling hand and pointed at the nearest bench. "The guards think I don't see their laziness in the way they leave their things around."

"Thank God for that," he said. He found the three-inch-long metal baton with a red light on one end. It was about an inch in diameter and had a handle section with grooves. Vahman turned his back to the bench and was able to grip the wand with one hand. He then returned to the door so Prita could see what he was doing.

"Tell me where I have to put it to loosen the ties," he said.

"To the left," she said. "A little up. More. There! Now press down hard, and when you feel it give, pull your hands out."

Vahman followed her instructions, and the minute the hard metal ties slacked around his wrist, he jerked free. When they fell to the floor, the metal immediately bunched together, tightening into a ball. He kicked it far away.

"Okay," he said, shaking his arms out. "Now how do I get you out?"

"I don't know," she whispered. She pointed to the keypad next to the door handle. "It's an old-fashioned keypad and not a digital one connected to the rest of the systems in the building. It's so if the power fails, this room can remain locked. I don't know the code."

"And the door is too heavy to break?"

She nodded.

"We're scientists, Prita," he said. "We can figure out a way to get through this. Tell me, how can I hack this thing?"

She closed her eyes, a tear leaking down her bruised face. "I have no idea."

"Then we'll have to see if there are any prints." He ran over to the section of the lab that had the powders and cleaning solutions. He found a container of cleaning powder and a brush. Then, he returned to the door.

"I have only ever seen this on TV back on earth," he

said. With as careful of a hand, he brushed it onto the keypad. Then he ran back to one of the benches and opened the drawers underneath the counter. He found a light, and after hitting the end a few times, it switched on. Vahman pointed it at the keypad.

"The numbers are six, nine, four, two, three, eight, seven. Is there an order that makes sense to you?"

She cocked her head to the left, then said, "Try nine, four, three, seven, six, eight, two."

He pressed the code, and there was a soft hiss before the door swung open, and Prita practically fell out into the hallway. Vahman dropped to his knees again to catch her.

"How did you know the code?" he asked.

"Brihaspathi coordinates," she whispered, her voice clear now that it wasn't separated by the glass. "My husband has an ego. He wants to own me as much as he wants to own everyone on Shukra."

Vahman helped her lean against the closed door and began feeling her arms and legs. "Dislocated shoulder, sprains maybe, plus cuts and bruises. Stay here." He raced to the right side of the lab, jumping over equipment he'd used time and time again, that he'd maintained for years. In the cabinet to the left of the entrance was storage shelving. He found Shukra first aid material. Then he ran to Prita's side and opened the kit.

"You're going to have to walk me through this. I have no idea what any of this does."

"This is the pain killer," she said, pointing to a transparent tab. "Hand it to me first."

He did, and she put the paper on her tongue. It immediately dissolved, and her body seemed to relax instantaneously. Then she loaded a syringe with a sedative and set it aside.

"Okay," she said, her voice calmer. "I'll need assistance in adjusting my shoulder."

He swallowed hard but followed her instruction as he gripped her bicep and, with one hard jerk, popped her shoulder back in place. Then he used the stich gun to sew her up, cleaning her wounds as he went. When they were done, it had been at least five minutes.

Prita let out a deep breath, her head falling back against the door she'd been locked behind for days. Her brow was damp with sweat. "I don't deserve your kindness," she whispered. "I locked you in a lab for years for the benefit of my people. You could've gone back to Earth, left me here to rot."

"No one can fault you for trying to save your people," he said. He leaned against the bench opposite of her, forearms resting on his knees. "You know what's really fascinating? Your sister has the same sense of duty."

"Shila," Prita said with a sigh. "My older didi. It's been so long, but I can still remember every moment with her. She's well?"

"She misses you, Prita. Did you know that she was the one funding the rebellion this whole time?"

Prita nodded. "She'd never leave me alone in my struggle. She helped the only way she could. She helped our people like a true Queen."

"She's coming for us."

Prita's eyes widened. "Is that how we're going to get out?"

"Yes," he said, smiling for the first time since he'd landed back on Shukra. "Because the Pirate Queen is probably angry right about now, and she's going to find me to let me know just how pissed she really is. Come on, let's find a better hiding place."

He stood, then looped her arm over his shoulder. "You know," he said, as they hobbled towards the tube elevator. "You should really invest in security that doesn't run the minute your husband shows up."

"He killed them all," Prita said hoarsely.

"And your sister will kill him. Now work with me. How do we get out of this lab?"

He watched her face, a study in concentration before her eyes lit up. "The tunnels. We created them to hide any of our children when the Brihaspathi landed on the planet. They're on the other side of the palace but we can get to them from a hidden corridor."

Vahman let out a low whistle. "I was here for seven years, and I never knew it was that easy for me to leave."

"It's not easy," Prita said softly. "But I'll keep you alive and get you out safely. I promised you all those years ago, and I intend on keeping my promises."

Vahman smiled. "Your sister would say the same thing."

CHAPTER 16

Of all the dumb, idiotic, stupid things Vahman could've done, he sacrificed himself to stay back in her ship, to send a sex tape and God knows what while she and her crew managed to get out.

What kind of absolute fool was he? And what exactly was he trying to do by putting himself in the line of fire? She could handle this situation on her own, and didn't need anyone's help, especially not from a *seeder*.

Shila landed the transport cruiser on the other side of the wall surrounding the family estate and immediately vacated it, running for the nearest brush so she wouldn't be caught. Then, accessing the opening she had used as a child, she entered the compound.

It was eerie seeing her family home again. She took a moment to look up at the side of the building where her bedroom used to be. Then she headed to the throne room. That was the place where her entire destiny changed.

Her timepiece buzzed, and she immediately removed the metal clasp on the side to insert it in her ear.

"Captain?" Fanna's voice said. "Do you copy?"

"Yes," she whispered.

"It looks like the human made the job easy for you. He is wearing a tracker we picked up. There is another one in what I think might be his tote bag that's currently in the possession of the Brihaspathi. The sound is disrupted. As for Vahman, he's on the lower level of the Shukra royal hall. Gabriella got the blueprints for it, and we can walk to the location."

"Is he safe for now?"

"I can't tell the extent of injuries, but based on what we're hearing, it's just him and Prita."

Prita. He was with Prita. Shila let out a breath. "Guide me to the second tracker. I'm going to take care of the Brihaspathi king first."

There was a hesitation on the other line, but Fanna agreed.

Shila slipped through the shadows, reliving triggering memories of her past as she moved from one familiar room to the next. The halls she ran through as a child, the archways that she would stand behind to hear her father sell Shukra after Shukra being. Then finally, she was sliding into the security wing off to the left of the royal hall. There was a guard out front, and she hid behind the drapes in the darkness until their back was turned. In two quick steps, she unsheathed her knife, and slit his throat. His blood sprayed in an arc over the tile, and a soft gurgling slipped from his lips as he choked on his own blood. Shila held him close until he stopped struggling, then lowered his body to the floor with a whisper.

After checking for any intruders in either direction, she opened the heavy double pane metal door of the security room, mindful of the cameras, before she slipped inside.

There were rows of computers, walls of screens and security footage, and the soft hum of machines.

A guard's voice interrupted the silence. "It looks like an old type of electronic device we'll have to plug in to download data. Humans. They are so primitive."

"I think we have an old fashion wire somewhere. Ah ha. There it is. Why don't you try this one?"

"Okay. Great, the ports fit, and...got it."

Two men sat in front of a wall of screens with Vahman's tablet in hand. So this wasn't where the Brihaspathi heir was but where they were reviewing the data for the contraceptive.

"Do you think he really came up with some sort of formula that protects breeders?"

"I hope not," the other man said. "Then breeders would be able to mate without getting pregnant, and we would lose our control over their activities. It is our divine right to have children, and their duty to serve us. There we go. It looks like it's downloading now."

Shila inched closer, checking to make sure her footsteps wouldn't set off any alarms, when the monitors in front of the two Brihaspathi guards turned black. The powered down, and then white noise cracked through the speakers. Seconds later, a familiar face appeared on all of the screens.

"My name is Dr. Vahman Raj."

The tape, Shila thought. They must've found it on the tablet. She waited in her crouched position until his monologue was over. She appeared on the screens next to the bed.

"Is that the heir to Shukra? Didn't she take an oath of celibacy?"

"Oh my gods," the second guard gasped. Shila grinned at the absolutely horrified sounds coming from the men.

"The contraceptive is real," one of them whispered.

At the first sound of her moan, she stood, and rested a hand on their shoulders. "I look fantastic, don't I?"

They spun in their seats, gaping at her like she was a ghost before she made quick work of knocking them out. She then removed their weapons and tied them up with the strange metal they had hooked in their waist bands. She pressed a finger to the piece in her ear.

"Security is down," she said. Then Shila exited the room as quietly as she'd entered. She strolled through the palace to the main hall, hiding behind drapery if she heard a sound. Based on what she'd seen so far, the Brihaspathi king would be sitting on her sister's throne where he didn't belong. When she rounded a corner, she saw that there were two guards at the entrance of the gold filigree doors.

She stepped out from her hiding spot, and when they noticed her, she had already drawn her laser gun and shot them in the center of their foreheads. They slumped to the ground before they could cry out in pain.

Then she shoved open the door, knives in both hands. "Brother-in-law! I heard you were looking for me."

The bastard who had hurt her baby sister sat in the same position her father used to sit, with his hubris cloaking him like a bad smell. He slowly got to his feet, his mouth set.

"I know I'm a little early, but I think it's time we had a chat—"

She heard the cries at that moment, and they sounded exactly like her own. Over her shoulder, hanging above the doors she'd just pushed open, was the recording of her mating with Vahman. It was the exact moment when she was on top, and Vahman's dick was going in and out of her cunt. It made her wet to even think about it now.

She'd assumed that the security guards had just downloaded the tape from the tablet, but no, this was everywhere, on all of the screens in the palace.

Vahman had done it. He'd sent the tape to the Intergalactic Congress, and it was now on every network in space.

"That," she said, pointing to the image of her pleasure, "is a real seeder. Even though I'm very upset with him right now."

The heir called out a command, and the four guards at his side drew their weapons as they moved on her. She had knives in their necks before they could point their laser shooters in her direction. As they fell like dominos around them, Prita's husband let out a roar.

To the sound of her orgasm, she approached this man, chin tilted up, head held high. "You hurt my baby sister," she said. "I owe Prita my life, and now I'm going to save hers."

"You're just another whore," he snapped, frothing at the mouth. "Your duty is to birth our children, and—"

"You don't want to piss me off," Shila said. "The last time I was in this room, I killed your brother because he got a little fresh and pissed me off, too. In fact, I think his body fell right over there."

The Brihaspathi scum roared like a fool. "You have absolutely no idea what you've done, and you will pay for—"

It took seconds to have a knife lodged in his neck. He gurgled, blood bubbling out the corner of his lips. Before he could get out a shot with the gun that he'd pulled from his waistband, she sprinted forward and with one quick slice, cut his head clean from his body. Purple blood spurt everywhere even as the sounds of her pleasure continued to echo through the hall, filling the silence.

Just as she finished the job, the doors swung open to more Brihaspathi guards, dozens of them now, with their weapons trained on her. She leaned down slowly and picked up the king's head by his hair and held it like a trophy. The expression on the face was the second of terror before it was separated from the rest of the body.

"The Intergalactic Congress knows what you've all done," she called out. "Leave. And take this with you." She tossed the head at the feet of the guards. They stared at her, and then the screen where Vahman was claiming his own pleasure buy pinning her to the mattress.

"I said leave otherwise you will be met with the same fate." This time, no one argued. They backed out of the hall, and Shila had to wonder how they became one of the strongest armies in the nine galaxies.

"Captain?" called the voice in her ear. "Is everything okay?"

"Cecil," she said, letting out a breath. "Tell me how to find that ridiculously stupid man and my sister."

There was a chuckle on the other end, but they gave her directions down to the labs on the lower level of the building, a place she hadn't even known existed when she lived here all those years ago, that Prita must've developed in the short time before Vahman had been taken.

When Shila reached the bottom level, the elevator shaft doors were wide open. She heard sounds of struggle, and she pulled her laser gun from its holster. Apparently, some of the troops weren't that stupid and decided to try their chance at kidnapping the two individuals in the lab for future negotiation. She would've done the same thing if she was honest with herself.

When she entered the lab, she saw two guards holding both Vahman and Prita by their necks with weapons against their temples, facing the doorway under which she stood.

"Drop your weapon!" one of them shouted.

"No," she replied.

The guards looked at each other, hesitating.

"She said 'no,'" Vahman repeated, and then jerked his head back to break the nose of the guard holding him.

The guard holding Prita captive also fell to the floor. Prita held up a syringe as she swayed on her feet. "This came in handy after all," she said. Then with her bruised face and broken body, she limped forward. Shila ran to her, jumping over debris until she could touch her sister.

"Your poor face," she whispered, knowing tears were streaming down her face now. She sobbed when Prita fell into her arms.

"Didi," Prita cried. And they were hugging each other, with Shila being as careful as she could with this delicate broken bird in her arms. Her heart was breaking at the realization that she had spent years like this.

"Is he dead?" Vahman said from behind Prita. There was a bruise forming on the corner of his lip. His hair was mussed.

"Yes," Shila said. "And you will be too once I'm done with you."

He smirked than wrapped his arms around both Shila and Prita. He pressed a kiss against Shila's forehead, and they stood together as a unit.

This could've been a lot worse, Shila thought. But

Vahman's faith in her ability to come and get them out had paid off.

There was a sound in the elevator shaft, a rumble that had the three of them springing apart. Shila motioned for Vahman to move Prita over behind the corner. She braced herself, and when the panel slid open, guards in white uniforms with guns drawn poured into the lab.

"We are the task force for the Intergalactic Congress," one of them said through a robotic face mask. "Drop your weapon now or we will shoot!"

Shila slid her knife back into her holster even as they ascended on her. "You don't want to shoot a member of the Shukra royal family, friends. I promise you, it's a bad look."

They all paused, then looked back and forth at one another. Prita emerged from hiding. "Stand down, soldiers," she said, her voice taking on an edge that Shila had never heard before.

"Queen Prita," one of them said, before genuflecting. "We've come to offer assistance. We received a distress message..."

"The Brihaspathi," she said. "They are the ones causing ah...*distress*."

"They are being escorted off your planet right now as we speak, and they won't be coming back," the solider replied. "We will also be issuing sanctions for their actions. There will be retribution."

Shila looked down at her sister, their eyes filling with tears. She didn't realize how emotional it would be to hear those words.

Free from their reign.

Free.

CHAPTER 17

The capital of Shukra was overrun by members of the Intergalactic Congress task force within hours of the Bhrihaspati king's execution. They took direction from Prita, and combed the streets to ensure that order was restored with the people. Prita released a planetary notice of martial law for a period of two weeks to regain order and control.

Vahman's call to one of the senior members had worked. More importantly, the Congress was now paying attention because everyone had seen the recording of the Pirate Queen's sexcapade.

Including Prita's husband's younger brother who was now the rightful ruler of Brihaspathi. Through the Intergalactic Congress, he'd sent a ship to retrieve Prita's husband's body. There was also a note.

I have your children. It's best if you negotiate in good faith if you'd like to see them alive, Queen Prita.

That night, Vahman had watched as Shila comforted her sister after receiving the note. They sat in Prita's quarters which was the only part of the palace that hadn't been defiled by the Brihaspathi.

"Tell me what I can do to help you," Shila said.

"Stand by my side. Both of you," she replied, then looked over at Vahman. "I will be addressing the Congress tomorrow morning."

They hadn't slept. There was too much to do, and the damage was widespread enough to make their safety questionable. But in the morning, Prita took her place in front of the palace communication panel, hands folded in front of her. Shila was to her left, while Vahman stood behind Shila.

The comms panel lit up, and Cecil helped connect the call.

Prita didn't bother trying to hide the bruises or the abuse the Brihaspathi had inflicted on her. She had said that she wanted the Congress to see what the Brihaspathi were capable of.

"Your sister has caused quite a stir," the elders said on the screen as the meeting began. They were obviously staring at the bandages and the dark bruises on her face. "What do you have to say to that, Queen Prita?"

Prita glanced back at Shila. "My sister was only doing what she felt she needed to do so you could understand the level of distress we were in. I have tried to obtain the aid of the Congress for years now, and we had no choice but to resort to drastic measures."

There was a pause, an uncomfortable silence on the other end of the communication panel. Prita had just accused the congress of aiding and abetting war crimes through their negligence against the Shukra people.

"Be that as it may, your scientist has done some remarkable work in creating a contraceptive that can protect all breeders," another elder said. "We will be sending members from all our galaxies to Shukra to obtain the formula—"

"You will not," Prita said.

There was rumbling now, and Vahman looked over at Shila, who shook her head in response in response.

"You deny us the science that can change all our worlds?" another voice cried.

"I don't deny you anything," Prita said. Her shoulders straightened, and Vahman watched as Prita's spine of steel made an appearance. "Shukra people are intelligent and resilient, but we've been taken advantage of for far too long. Senators, centuries ago, when space travel was invented, invading planets colonized my people. The first crime was committing mass genocide of all of our Shukra seeders. Then our breeders were raped and sold generation and after generation. Our children ripped from our arms—" her voice cracked, and Shila reached out to put a hand on her shoulder. "No, senators. We will be developing the contraceptive to ensure that anyone who needs it, will have access. We plan on expanding our research to support breeder bodies beyond contraceptives as well."

There was more silence, until finally someone said, "I believe that is fair considering all the time, money, and effort the Shukra put into developing the contraceptive in the first place. You will…sell your contraceptive then."

Prita nodded. "First, there is much to do to recover from the Brihaspathi damage on my planet. My children—" She coughed, and Vahman could feel the pain as if it was a living, breathing entity in the air. "My children are trapped on Brihaspathi. My oldest is ten and I haven't seen them since they were born. Family, and my people will be my first priority. Then once our labs are up and running again, I will be happy to report method of purchase and facilitation to governments wishing to have the contraceptive on hand."

There were a few matriarch figures on the screen, and they met Prita's speech with genuine smiles.

"Because we have failed you for so long, please let us know what we can do now to make up for our error and support your people as you heal," one of them said. "Until then, we will be waiting eagerly for your report."

The connection ended and Prita slumped, as if weighed down from the heaviness of her responsibility. Shila reached her first, wrapping her up in her arms.

"You are so brave, Prita."

"So are you," she said, her voice shaking. Prita then turned to Vahman.

"Thank you. Without the completed contraceptive, we would've still been under the control of the Brihaspathi that my parents forced on us so long ago."

He shook his head. "I didn't do as much as you think. It was actually your research that got me thinking about how to put the puzzles together." It had been so easy once he'd seen the way Prita's experiment results matched his.

Prita looked at Sana first, then back at Vahman. "I know this is not something that you would ever consider, but you are welcome to come stay in the labs to lead a team..."

Vahman was already shaking his head. "I gave you copies of the research. You should be able to replicate it easy enough. Once you ramp up production, you'll need a steady supply of human antibodies, but I'm sure that can be retrieved from Earth. If you have any questions about the findings, you can reach me and I'm happy to answer them, but I'm only here as long as Shila is here. I plan on traveling with your sister."

Both Shila and Prita's eyes widened. Prita turned to Shila. "It goes without saying that your exile has been revoked. I would love to have my sister rule by my side here."

Shila reached out to hold Prita's hands. "I'm sorry, but I think too much time has passed. It's good to know that I'm able to return home to check in on you whenever I can which is all that I want. My hope is to open a port town in the Rahu, close to Earth. Once I've completed enough missions to pay the Congress for my port town, and I'm able to begin construction, then I hope you come visit me."

Prita tilted her head in a move so like Shila's that Vahman had to hold back a smile. "How much money do you need?" Prita asked.

"I don't plan on borrowing from my sister—"

"You wouldn't be borrowing," Prita interrupted. She sounded every bit of a ruler as she'd been on the call with Congress. "You've earned an inheritance that was supposed to be issued upon your marriage. I wasn't able to touch it for the rebellion because it would gotten my husband's attention. This is your money, Shila."

Shila bit her lower lip. "How much inheritance are we talking about?"

Prita named a figure that had Shila gaping. "How is it possible that our inheritance is that much money?"

It clicked for Vahman first. "It's not really an inheritance," he said. "It's a dowry, isn't it? It's part of the fee that your parents received when they sold you to the Brihaspathi, and it's supposed to keep you comfortable."

Prita nodded. "He's right."

"Then I'll take it," Shila said. "Every last fucking cent

of it. And I'll register the port town as soon as possible so that we can ship supplies back to Shukra for your contraceptive production."

The sisters continued to talk and make plans for the future, touching constantly as if they were worried, they would be ripped apart again any minute. Vahman stood watch in silence, and when they were done, he escorted Shila back to her ship for one last night of sleep on Shukra.

CHAPTER 18

Shila knew that she was avoiding talking about it, but it was time to have a conversation with Vahman about their future. It had taken a few days, but she worked with the rest of her crew to load up on supplies from food to fuel. She then went through all of the repairs herself to make sure that her ship was fully functional. Once everything was ready, she gave her crew two hours to say their goodbyes to old families and friends while she walked the halls of her ship alone in search of her own goodbye.

She found Vahman in the Captain's Dome staring out at the landscape through the open window. His arms were crossed, and he wore a fresh pair of Shukra clothes from his tunic to his shoes. His hair, slightly long, curled at the base of his neck. There was a small tablet in his hand that Shila knew his sister had gifted him. He was writing questions and what looked like equations when she walked up to stand behind him.

"Hey," she said.

Vahman turned in his seat and smiled at her warmly. "Hey," he said. "The ship is all packed up?"

"Yes," Shila replied. She swallowed the lump in her throat. "Vahman, we're ready to take off. I know what you said before we fought the Brihaspathi, but are you still interested in staying on board or do you want to go home? We can still take you back to Earth." It was better to ask him outright, to just deliver the question and hope the wound his response would cause wouldn't bleed for too long.

Vahman raised a brow. "I know we haven't been together long, but you should know by now that I say what I mean, Shila." He held out a hand for her, and she didn't hesitate to take it. He pulled her down on his laugh, the grunted at the impact of her ass hitting his thighs.

His poor bone density was nowhere near that of a Shukras. Shila shifted so that she could support some of her wait on her feet that she'd kept flat on the ground. Then she combed her fingers through his hair. Their faces were close together. His tablet was now resting on the dashboard next to the control panel.

"You've wanted Earth for so long," she whispered.

"I've wanted family for so long," he replied. "And now I have it."

He pressed a gentle kiss against her mouth, and he sighed against the feeling of his touch. This seeder was one that she could trust. She knew that now.

When she pulled back, he cupped her jaw in his hand. "I am looking forward to learning all of your secrets, Shila."

"Human, I can't wait to learn more of yours."

They looked out at the Shukra landscape together.

Construction units had already moved in to start modernizing the capital. Some of the money had been donated directly from the palace coffers, while the rest had been from the taxes that remained untouched after the Brihaspathi took over. Prita had been concerned about using it because she was sure her husband would take it away from the people when it was meant for infrastructure, schools, government buildings and revitalization. She'd been careful to hide the financial stability of Shukra from his greedy eyes.

There was also a series of investments that were coming in from senators in the congress interested in funding research for their own races. Shukra had started to develop an identity, a name for brilliance in healthcare.

"Prita is a good leader," Shila said quietly. "But she's so broken. Such terrible things have happened to her. I hope this gives her purpose."

"I gave her the red vial," Vahman said. "The one you'd given me to jump back in time and space."

Shila sat up, ignoring his grunt. "*What*? I thought that was destroyed when the Brihaspathi confiscated your bag."

"No," Vahman replied. "I kept it tucked in my shoe. I told Prita if she wanted to go back to the before, then she'd have a way to relive her life without consequence. She says she might think about it."

"If anyone deserves another chance, it's Prita," Shila said. She thought of her sister's bruises again, and then of Vahman's stolen life. "But if she has the vial, Vahman, that means you don't ever have a chance of going back."

He pulled her into his arms. She tucked her head against the crook of his neck and wrapped her arms around his waist.

"Shila," he whispered. "I made my choice. We may

have just met, but I know that I want to travel with you, explore with you, set up that port town. There was a part of you that tugged at a part of me since before we met. And that's why I was so mad when I couldn't figure out why you had left your sister. The question is, now that we're no longer in danger, are you willing to give me a chance?"

How could she say no to that? She'd spent so much of her life running from her past, running from the people who threatened her choices, and the rights to her own body. Now they were free, and she wanted to be with this seeder, with this man who was willing to run into danger to make sure that she had a chance.

She leaned back so she could see his face. "Just so we're clear, I'll always be the Captain of this ship, and the monarch of my port town."

He grinned, and then pressed a kiss to the tip of her nose. "Yes, my Pirate Queen. I'll follow you wherever you want to lead me. As long as we're together."

EPILOGUE

Prita let Nemi into her private quarters in the middle of the night. This was the first time since Shukra's freedom that she'd accepted an offer for pleasure from a fellow breeder. It was time. Her broken bones and scars had healed, and now her heart had to heal, too. But the mating wasn't going according to plan.

As lovers went, Nemi was beautiful and a fine choice. He possessed a wide frame, a dreamy face and bright brown eyes accentuated by the ring of gold.

After a few moments of awkwardness, he led her to the bed covered in the softest fabrics their planet had to offer. He stroked her body, touching and kissing her neck. She tried to reciprocate but wasn't interested enough to do more than run her hands over his naked arms as she rested her head against her pillows. Then he pulled her nightgown out of the way and separated her legs. Nemi kissed her between her pussy lips, pausing there as if waiting for her to react. When she let out a small sigh, he kissed the inside of her knee and sat up.

"Your highness?"

She knew they had barely begun but she wasn't growing wet with anticipation. No, in fact she was bored. After debating whether or not she should let Nemi stay, she closed her legs and sat up.

"That's enough," she said softly. "That's enough for tonight."

He slipped off the end of the bed and stood shirtless in the darkness. "I'm so sorry I couldn't satisfy you," Nemi said, his head bowed.

"No, Nemi it wasn't you," she said as she tugged her lace Shukra attire into place. The gown was sheer except for the fauna patterns that covered her nipples and the apex of her thighs. "I believed I was ready, but I don't think I am just yet. When it is time for me to try again, I will call you. But for now, please leave me so I can rest."

"I don't mean to pry," Nemi said, hesitating as he pulled on his shirt. "But is it your children you are thinking of? We know that you miss them..."

Yes, she thought. Always. Their baby faces, scrunched in angry tears before they were ripped from my arms, are all forever imprinted on my brain.

"I always think of my children," she said softly. "Thank you, Remi. You may go."

"Yes, my queen. And when you are ready, I look forward to bringing you pleasure."

Nemi bowed then exited Prita's quarters through the titanium double doors.

She was finally alone again.

Prita thought of her sister as she adjusted her pillow. If Shila was here, would she have wanted Prita to pretend to be interested in Nemi so she could finish? In theory, Prita could call Shila to ask if she'd done the right thing, but she didn't want to intrude. No, Shila

was building her port town on the floating island of Dwarka, named for the lost Shukra city that plunged into the sea. She was living with her scientist, Vahman, and creating new trade routes for their people and the contraceptive they developed.

In truth, Shila was having an adventure because she was so much braver than Prita could ever be.

With the memory of her sister in her mind, and thoughts of how Prita would one day be just as brave to stand up to the Brihaspathi and reclaim her children, she closed her eyes with every intention of getting her rest so she could rule another day.

A voice cut through the darkness. "He will never be able to give you pleasure."

Prita gasped, jerking into a sitting position. "Who's there?" she called out.

The overhead illuminator brightened the corner of her room. A man with stark white hair, an imposing body, and a face etched in sinful cruelty stared back at her. He wore thick leather pants, combat boots, and toyed with a long, serrated blade in one hand.

"Hello, your majesty."

She began to tremble. The Brihaspathi.

"How did you get here," she said, even as she inched closer to the bedside table. If she could reach the hidden alarm, then she'd be able to call for help. She needed to alert her guards.

"I wouldn't touch that button if I were you."

She stopped inching forward. Her voice shook as she spoke. "The Brihaspathi have committed war crimes against my people. You are not welcome."

"My brother committed those crimes," he said as he stood, reaching his full height. He was taller than her by two hands length. "You and I have never met, even though your children are in my care."

At the mention of her children, she got to her knees and wrapped her arms across her breasts. "What happened to my babies?"

"Nothing," he said smoothly. She knew the room was bright enough that he would be able to see her in all her vulnerability, but there something about the way he looked at her that didn't strike the same fear that she always felt in the presence of her husband. With the former king, she'd curled into herself. She stayed quiet and avoided moving to draw attention to herself. This man looked like he expected her to fight.

"What do you want?" she said evenly.

"So many things, your majesty," he said as he swaggered across the room. When he reached her bedside, he used the flat end of his knife to lift her chin so that she looked directly at him. The metal was cool, and she felt the sharp edges prick her ever so lightly. "But first, stop shaking. A queen does not cower."

His words sparked an anger so strong that she burned from it. She dropped her hand, her gown parting as she stood on her knees. "I do not cower from the likes of Brihaspathi."

He looked down at her breasts, and to her shock, he used his knife to further part her gown so that the fabric pooled at her sides. Her nipples and her pussy were fully exposed. Along with the burning anger for his brazen intrusion was the first hint of desire. What was wrong with her? She abhorred the Brihaspathi, especially someone who was related to the man who had brutalized her for years. But the thought of him touching her was frighteningly erotic. Was this how her body betrayed her?

"How dare you come to my private quarters and taunt me?" she whispered, squaring her shoulders. "Do you think you know my desires better than I do? Because you're a seeder?" she sneered. Even as she spoke, Prita pressed her thighs together, feeling an ache in her lower belly. Her guards were forgotten.

"Queen Prita." Those bright blue eyes focused on hers. "I know that you'll need more than whatever that softhand breeder could've offered."

She could feel her nipples tighten at the intensity of his stare. "Ahh," he said, as if her body's reaction was the answer he was looking for. "You know this, too. That's why you are feeling desire with someone like me."

He sheathed his knife and removed the holster from his hip. He placed it on the bedside table. To her shock, he toed off his boots then began unbuttoning his crisp white tunic.

"W-what are you doing?" she said. She felt herself grow damp at the sight of his muscled chest. His biceps and forearms flexed as he shrugged out of his shirt.

"I am giving you the pleasure you need, your majesty," he said as the tunic fell to the floor. "That pathetic guard who didn't even register my presence will never be able to fuck you the way I am about to."

"It will be a cold day on Shukra before I ever let another Brihaspathi touch me," she whispered. Her legs trembled in anticipation.

As if accepting the dare, this trailed his fingertips down her collarbone and over the curve of her breast. His touch roughened as he gripped the sides of her gown and yanked it off her shoulders and down her arms. She gasped, feeling the thrill rush through her. She was naked now, her body on full display.

He would be able to see all the scars, the stretch marks, and the pulled skin at her abdomen from her pregnancies. Good, she thought. Let him know what his brother had done.

When he reached out to touch her again, she pulled back and slapped him across the face as hard as she could so that his head snapped to the left. The sound was like a crash, and the pain from the impact stung her red, throbbing palm.

This man lifted a finger to the corner of his mouth and touched the bluish blood that bubbled from the small cut. Like a mad man, he chuckled. "I will deny your orgasm for five minutes longer now."

He moved lightening quick and gripped the hand that had struck him. She tugged hard, struggling to break the contact, but she was a scientist, and he was a warrior. In strength, he'd win. He pried her fingers open so that he could inspect her palm, and then he leaned down to press a kiss to the center of the bright red spot that had made an impact against his cheek. His stubble tickled her skin.

"You can use these fingers in a more useful manner," he said. He then cupped the back of her head and pulled her towards him, so their lips were a hair's length apart. "Touch yourself now."

His lips brushed against hers as he spoke. "The same fingers that had hurt me. Use them to excite your cunt. I need you wet for my cock."

"N-no," she whispered, even as her fingertips began stroking the throbbing clitoris at the top of her pussy lips. She could feel her wetness growing with each jagged breath. Images of his stark white hair between her legs flashed in her mind. "Who are you?"

He kept his eyes locked on hers as he unbuckled his belt. "I am Vicktor, King of the Brihaspathi people, and you have killed my one surviving family member."

She gasped when Vicktor removed her hand from her pussy, then slipped her fingers between his lips. An unexplainable moan escaped from her mouth as she felt his tongue and the pressure of his sucking as he licked her fingers clean.

He toppled her back against the bed, then whipped off his belt. His pants fell to the floor, and he was now completely undressed. In the dim light, Prita saw the ridged lines of his long, hard cock. Anticipation had her gasping and writhing against the sheets for the first time in her life. She wanted this. She wanted him to punish her, to fuck her hard and she wanted to fight.

"Have you taken this infamous contraceptive?" he said calmly as he climbed onto the bed. "Or will I plant my seed in your womb for you to have a child that is mine?"

"I do not want another child," she snapped. "I have taken the contraceptive."

He parted her thighs and rubbed the tip of his cock against her pussy lips. "That's too bad," he said as he notched the tip against her hole. "I would've liked to breed you, Queen Prita. See you swollen with our young."

She gasped as he pushed in a fraction of a bit farther. "I'll only ask you again one more time," she panted. "W-what do you want?" Vicktor gripped wrists then pinned them above her head. Prita was now soaked, all thoughts of Nemi gone from her mind. She watched as that cruel mouth curved in a smile that could only be described as sinister.

"I want revenge," he whispered. "And I'm going to take it by having you." He slammed his hips forward and thrust his cock so deep that Prita screamed. She wrapped her legs around his waist and hooked her ankles at the small of his back as he began to fuck her in hard, powerful thrusts that had her straining against him.

This, she thought. This was what it was supposed to be like. This was how it was supposed to be. Prita's mind became hazy, and even though she knew that she should fear this man, she held on to the power that he gave her, the pleasure that coursed through her. It was as if she was untouched before this moment, reveling in the strength of her body. Her breasts bounced with each powerful thrust, her skin slick with sweat as Vicktor fucked her over and over and over again until they gasped for breath.

Then at the precipice of her orgasm, he pressed his mouth against her ear and whispered words that struck both fear and lust in her heart. "Queen Prita, you made a mistake. Now this cunt belongs to me."

THE SHUKRA DUOLOGY

After years of pain and sacrifice, Prita is finally able to dream of a peaceful future for herself and her people. Except her children are still with the Brihaspathi. She must negotiate with the new ruler who replaced her dead husband in an effort to get them back.

Except the price he asks is too high for her to pay.

To find out when you can read Prita's story, follow Nina Saxena's newsletter found on her Website, and Instagram for the latest updates.